A Christmas
to Remember

Tales of Comfort and Joy

Scholastic Canada Ltd.

Introduction copyright © by Scholastic Canada Ltd. All rights reserved.
The stories in this book are the copyrighted property of their respective authors.
See page 248 for continuation of copyright information.
Published by Scholastic Canada Ltd.
SCHOLASTIC and DEAR CANADA and logos are trademarks
and/or registered trademarks of Scholastic Inc.

Library and Archives Canada Cataloguing in Publication

A Christmas to remember : tales of comfort and joy.

(Dear Canada)
ISBN 10 0-545-99003-3/ISBN 13 978-0-545-99003-5

1. Canada--History--Juvenile fiction. 2. Christmas stories, Canadian
(English). 3. Children's stories, Canadian (English).
I. Series: Dear Canada

PS8323.C57 C58 2009   jC813'.081083271   C2009-901194-8

6 5 4 3 2 1   Printed in Canada   09 10 11 12 13

The display type was set in BernhardMod BdIt BT.
The text was set in Goudy Old Style BT.

First printing June 2009

Table of Contents

Introduction

The publication of our new Christmas anthology and our 25th Dear Canada book definitely makes this a Christmas to remember. Close to a million Dear Canada books have found homes across the country, featuring diarists from as long ago as 1666 with the arrival of the *filles du roi,* and from all parts of Canada — Vancouver Island to Newfoundland, southern Ontario to Hudson Bay. The letters we receive, and the responses to the Dear Canada website, tell us how much you enjoy these books.

When we published *A Season for Miracles,* thousands of you reconnected with girls you had grown to love. In this new anthology, you'll enjoy reading about other Dear Canada diarists as they experience "the Christmas after" — Fiona Macgregor from *If I Die Before I Wake,* Anya Soloniuk from *Prisoners in the Promised Land,* Julia May Jackson from *A Desperate Road to Freedom,* and eight others. You'll find old friends here, and maybe a new one from a Dear Canada book you haven't even read yet. I hope you'll enjoy letting these wonderful girls, and their challenges and triumphs, into your life once again.

Happy Christmas, and Happy Reading,
Sandra Bogart Johnston, Editor, Dear Canada Series

Fiona Macgregor

If I Die
Before I Wake

The Flu Epidemic Diary
of Fiona Macgregor

Toronto, Ontario
August 3, 1918–March 22, 1919

BY JEAN LITTLE

*During the euphoria towards the end of World War I,
a different enemy stalked the land, killing by the
hundreds and thousands. First Fee's twin Fanny,
then her older sister Jemma, caught the dreaded
Spanish Flu. Fee's family struggled to pick up the pieces,
to put the War behind them, to face an even deadlier
enemy. But there is now one bright spot
on the Macgregor family's horizon.*

Untangling Christmas

Sunday, December 5, 1920

Dear Ben,

About an hour ago, Aunt handed me this little book and told me she wants me to write the story of your first Christmas because you will be too young to remember it.

I asked her why she did not write it herself. She said that I was the only one in the family who was a true writer, and that she was too busy preparing all the Christmas foods and presents and decorations we would need to help us have a happy holiday in spite of everything.

I will begin by introducing us. You are my half BROTHER, because we have the same father, and you are my COUSIN because your mother is also my aunt. Mother and Aunt were twins, like Fanny and me and Jo and Jemma. Mother died when Theo, your big brother, was born, and Aunt stayed with us to bring us up. Then, years later, Father and Aunt got married and finally, Benjamin, you were born. It sounds complicated, and I even had a hand in making it happen. But all that matters right now is that I am your sister Fee, you are my brother Ben, and you will have your first birthday on Boxing Day.

I have always loved Christmas. I think I have loved it even better than Fan's and my birthday. There is so much more to it and everybody is included. But this year it seems tangled. Christmas is not supposed to be all snarled up, filled with unhappiness and difficulty, but that is how this coming one feels to me.

It is as though I got out our box of decorations, filled to the brim with spools of bright ribbon and blown-glass bulbs and shining tinsel, but when I lifted off the lid, I found everything had grown faded and frayed. Maybe explaining it that way sounds foolish. But it is just how it seems. I feel as though I am about to burst out crying. But I must do no such thing. This book is not supposed to be filled with mournful moans. It is meant to tell you about your first birthday.

Ben, Aunt must truly like my writing. Otherwise she would not ask me to do this. This thought just lit a fat spark of joy inside me and almost banished my bad mood. I do love writing. Perhaps writing this Birthday Book for you will be fun, after all. I will begin tomorrow. Ignore this first bit. It doesn't count.

Dear Ben,

I am going to begin even though I am feeling down in the dumps again. It is very hard for me to write when I am in this state. I just want to go to bed and pull the covers over my head and block out the world and everyone in it. I wonder if Aunt guesses I feel grumpy, gloomy and glum. Probably. She has always been able to see inside me.

Usually when December comes I bounce about, full of joy and excitement. I love choosing presents and giving them, and getting them too, of course. I love the carols and the special foods and reading Christmas stories. Theo helps by counting down the days. The Christmas before our sister Jemma died, he actually counted the hours at the end.

Jemma died of the Spanish Flu two years ago. It was just before Christmas and we had a hard time celebrating. We did our best for Theo, though. He was too little to understand our grief. Last year we all went to Grandy and Grandma's farm the day before Christmas Eve and did not leave until Boxing Day morning. Being away made everything different and easier somehow.

Then the minute we walked in our door, Aunt said she thought maybe Father should call the doctor. You were not due until February, Ben, so nobody had given you a thought. But you were in a hurry and you were born at eight o'clock that very evening. I remember staring at you in amazement. I had never seen a human being so small and yet so special. Nobody could feel sad after you came. We were all too busy. Father said you must have known we needed you sooner than we planned.

But this year we will be home. And not only will we be missing Jemma terribly, but Jo is going to be away too. She and her friend Carrie agreed to help put on a Christmas shindig for poor families. Personally, I believe we ourselves will be a poor family without my big sisters. When Jemma was alive, she and Jo always made the holiday so jolly.

I know. We have *you* now to help cheer us up. But one baby, however dear, cannot take the place of two big girls. Theo has his dog to help keep his mind occupied, at least.

I wonder if Jo still misses Mother the way I miss Jemma. I remember Mother, of course, but not clearly. Seven years is a long time. I know her favourite carol was "O, come all ye faithful."

There is something else wrong, Ben. Fanny seems almost like a stranger these days. I used to know her every thought, but then the Gibsons moved here and Connie and Fan have grown thick as thieves. I try to be polite but I can't think why Fan likes her.

She never passes a mirror without stopping to gaze at herself.

Oh, I cannot write any more today.

Tuesday, December 7, 1920

Dear Ben,

It is almost bedtime and dark out, but Fanny has gone for a walk with her Bosom Friend Constance. They giggle all the time and lean close to whisper secrets, mostly about boys. And they try so hard to be stylish.

Am I jealous, Ben? I never was before. We shared everything, even our friends.

I am tired and I would like to go to bed, but I can't sleep while Fan is out. Aunt says that is foolish. I told her it is because Fan and I are twins, but she reminded me that she and my mother were twins too. I hardly ever think of them that way.

Fan called back over her shoulder to say I should come too. She knows I feel left out but she also knows I think Con is silly. I did not tell her but she knows. When I said I was busy, Connie snickered.

Anyway, Ben, two is company. Three is a crowd.

Aunt made Christmas pudding today. The whole house smelled lovely. So rich and fruity. I kept licking my lips.

There, I am supposed to put Christmassy things in

this book for you, and now I have.

Theo wants me to check the spelling on his Christmas list. I told him Santa Claus did not mind spelling mistakes, but your brother does not want to take a chance. This book will get better soon, Ben. I promise. At least I got the smell of the pudding in.

Wednesday, December 8, 1920

Dear Ben,

Aunt decided I looked peaked at breakfast and kept me home from school. Fanny was outraged, which pleased me. I am sitting on the couch to write this and you are sitting in your playpen right in front of me. You keep finding toys to throw at me but I am pretending to be so busy writing in your book and reading the paper that I don't notice.

The paper tells about all the men out of work right now, thousands of them in Toronto alone. There is going to be a big march tomorrow. It is terrible that men came home from the War to find no jobs waiting.

Aunt just took you away for your nap. Maybe I'll have one too.

Same day, afternoon

I wonder, Ben, if you like Fanny better than me.

I did not mean to write that, but it is true. I don't mean you hate me, but babies don't hide their feelings, and you grin and wave your hands whenever she looks your way. I just know "Fan" will be your first word. If she were here, she would take you out of your cage and play with you, but she is not home yet, so you must put up with me. I wonder if writing to you this way will help us get to know each other better.

We just took a break for milk and cookies. It is lucky that I like rusks. Not slobbered on, though. I am sorry I would not take the bite you offered me, but it was disgusting.

All right. I will stop writing and show you the pictures of toys in the Eaton's catalogue — after I wipe that mush off your face.

Thursday, December 9, 1920

The newspaper said that those men did march yesterday, Ben. Hundreds of them.

Cooking Break.

Fanny called me to come and make fudge. It was so nice doing it together. You loved the "soft balls" we gave you. My arm aches from beating that bowl of fudge, but it was worth it. We made lots. Yum!

Now Aunt is putting you to bed. Sleep well, little one.

Friday, December 10, 1920

Dear Ben,

I'm feeling better today so I took you out for a ride in your baby sled after school. You looked cuter than any of the children in the Eaton's catalogue. Your cheeks got so red and your eyes so bright. And you kept waving your arms and shouting baby words.

I do love you, little Ben. You cheer me up.

Saturday, December 11, 1920

Dear Ben,

Today is more exciting for you because Theo has gone skating and left Hamlet to keep us company. Hamlet, being a Great Dane, is about fifty times as big as you. He lies with his enormous face pushed up to the bars of the playpen so he can watch your every move. He seems to know that when you smack his head, you mean it lovingly. He's snoring now and you think it is hilarious. You are both clowns.

I am supposed to write about *you*, Ben, but you want me to stop and show you the catalogue again. You sure can get your message across. All right. We can look at the children's clothes right now.

Book Break.

Aunt has just taken you away to change your diaper. While you are gone, I will write a bit more. It is tricky trying to write about a baby and play with him at the same time. Maybe you will take your first step when you are with me. I wish you would. That would show Miss Fanny. She's spent the entire day with Connie and never given Aunt a lick of help.

Not that I have been such a saint.

Sunday, December 12, 1920

Dear Ben,

I am not in a writing mood. Why did I promise your mother I would tell you everything about your first Christmas? I should have known better.

We are back together, you in the playpen, Hamlet keeping guard and myself writing and grumbling.

Why am I so grumpy, you ask? Fan has gone out for a walk with Con and Wendell Bowman. I do not like Wendell Bowman. He acts as though Fanny is his private property. He is three years older than she is. It is called "robbing the cradle"! I can't believe he is seriously stuck on her.

That is enough for today.

Monday, December 13, 1920

Dear Benjamin,

Today I discovered how precious you are to me. After I came home from school I spread out a blanket on the living room floor so you would be able to have more freedom. Then the doorbell rang. It was a man wanting Father. Then I took time to run to the bathroom for a moment. After all, you usually crawl backwards and you do it slowly. So I was sure you were safe. Yet when I came back you were gone!

I did not believe it. I looked all over. You were NOWHERE to be found.

Fanny had taken you, of course. She actually took you OUTSIDE to introduce you to her friend Wendell. She did not even put on your coat and mittens or wrap you up in a shawl. When she came back, your little cheeks were so red and your fingers were almost blue.

"Wendell says he's adorable," she cooed, plunking you down on the blanket and dashing back outside.

Oh, Ben, I feel as though I've lost Fanny as well as Jemma and Jo.

Tuesday, December 14, 1920

Dear Ben,

I got my bangs trimmed. The rest still goes down to my shoulders. Fanny and I look less identical now. I am taller since she was so sick with that flu. Also I wear specs now because I am short-sighted. You would think Fanny would need them too, but she says she can see perfectly. She had her hair cut in a proper bob ages ago, with disgusting kiss curls on her cheeks and a fringe down to her eyebrows. She said my haircut is nice, but I could tell she thought it was boring. I know it isn't stylish, but I don't want to be stylish.

Or do I? Once in a blue moon, maybe. But not really.

Aunt says to be patient and that "I will come into my own." Whatever that means.

I wish Jo was home more and had time to talk. Since Jemma died, Jo is changed. I guess I would be too if anything happened to Fan. But Jo has moved into a world of medical students and studying and being busy.

I should remember to tell you some Christmas news, Ben. It is ten days from tomorrow. I know because Theo keeps reminding us all. Aunt hung the evergreen wreath on the front door. Soon we will put up our tree.

Wednesday, December 15, 1920

Dear Ben,

I had just got settled down to write to you when Fanny came rushing in and ran straight upstairs.

Father marched in right behind her, muttering something about her looking like a hussy with that muck all over her face. I waited, and after he went into his study she came down with her face scrubbed clean and her eyes red. I could hear Connie and Wendell outside, laughing their heads off.

"Fan, listen to them," I said.

She stood still for a second, long enough to hear them. Then she glared at me and ran back out. I wonder if they went on making fun of her even after she got there.

Oh, Ben, I do feel sorry for Fan. She has other friends, better ones, but she seems to have dropped them totally since Connie and Wendell came along.

I will stop writing now and play with you for a bit. Theo should be here any minute too and he can join in. We are teaching you Patty Cake, Patty Cake. I remember teaching it to Theo.

Thursday, December 16, 1920

Dear Ben,

Soon you will be able to do Patty Cake. I am very proud of the way you keep trying. You wrinkle up your face and stare at me and Theo and smack your hands together and make noises. You're almost there.

After supper

Fanny has been invited to go to the Seniors' Christmas Dance and Aunt says she is too young. Fan is beside herself. She is actually *yelling* at Aunt. What has come over her? She thinks she is being a Flapper. I think she is being a pain in the neck.

Oh, Ben, Fanny and I have always been so close! I cannot bear this coldness between us, especially right at Christmas. She's going to get her heart broken. Why doesn't she see what they are really like?

Friday, December 17, 1920
In the middle of the night

Dear Ben,

After we went to bed, Fanny got up and sneaked out of the house in the dark. Father and Aunt had gone to their room and Theo was sound asleep. Hamlet gave one deep growl, but I was the only one to hear him. I got up and looked out the window and saw Connie waiting. Fan was gone for half an hour!

I pretended to be asleep when she came in but she knew I wasn't. She got into bed without turning on a light. Then I heard her sniffle. She was crying. I waited a while and then I asked what was wrong.

"None of your business," she said.

I just waited. I knew she'd tell. Then she said

Wendell was so furious that she couldn't go to the dance, he asked Con, and Con said yes.

Well, Ben, I knew Wendell was a rotter, but I am still sorry for Fan.

"I hate him," she finished. Then she whispered, "I hate them both."

That is good news, Ben. She went to sleep after that. But I didn't. I shouldn't be writing this in your book, but I can't tell Father or Aunt, and Jo is not around.

You'd think I was Fan's mother instead of her sister. But her mother is dead and Aunt is busy with Christmas and her baby Ben.

I am going back to bed and, I hope, to sleep.

Saturday, December 18, 1920

Dear Ben,

Christmas is less than a week away. Yet I hear Aunt singing downstairs, and instead of singing carols she is warbling "I'll be with you in apple blossom time." I will sing something to remind her that this is WINTER.

Fifteen minutes later

I started in on "God rest ye merry, gentlemen." Aunt broke off. Then I heard her laugh. Now she is singing "Jingle Bells." That's more like it.

Con came by but Fanny had gone out to do Christmas shopping. "Tell her I came by," said Connie with a big smirk. I did *not* promise. I think Fanny partly went early so she would not be here if Con came.

Fan said I could not come with her. She must be buying my present. What do you suppose it is, Ben?

I got *you* a ball made of cloth and a set of alphabet blocks. They are perfect.

Fanny just came in and shot upstairs with parcels to hide. And her old friend Margery was with her. I can hear them talking a mile a minute. Oh my, Ben, things are improving by leaps and bounds.

Sunday, December 19, 1920

Dear Ben,

At church, they asked me to help out in the nursery. You were so good. Betsy Walker yelled her head off when she hit her nose on the bar of the playpen, and you crawled over and patted her and made soft comforting sounds until she smiled. We taught the older ones "Away in a Manger." Well, we sang it to them and they sort of hummed along.

It seems such a happy time, but one of the teachers was crying because her husband still has no job even though he's been back from the War for nearly a year.

Another of the teachers made me feel selfish for being excited about Christmas coming. She says her children will have presents because they have grandparents to help out, but lots of children won't. I wish we could help, Ben, but thousands of men must have hundreds and hundreds of children. I'll ask Father.

Monday, December 20, 1920

Dear Ben,

Father and Theo brought home a tree. It smells wonderful. We set it up, with lots of trials and errors, and it is halfway decorated.

I brought up the subject of the men with no jobs and the children without presents. I knew we could not help many, but maybe we could help ONE family if we knew of one.

"We'll think about it, Fiona," Father said, looking serious and pleased at the same time.

I am very hopeful. Good night.

Tuesday, December 21, 1920

Dear Ben,

Our whole house smells like a forest!

The minute Father finished asking the grace at supper, Aunt told us that she had found a family that needed our help. "I had a feeling you would," Father said, beaming at her. Aunt told us that a woman was at the library this morning when she was taking back our books. The woman had come in to get warm and she was looking so despairing that Aunt struck up a conversation with her. Her sister's family has nothing. The woman herself said she could not manage to help out, because she has four children of her own and her husband lost his leg in the War. Anyway, Aunt said she knew right away that here was our chance, so she kept talking until she learned where the family lived, and all the children's names and ages. She moved to another table and scribbled them down to be sure.

Suddenly Theo said, "There are lots of presents piling up in the living room. Maybe we could share. I would be willing to give my new striped pyjamas."

"How do you know you have new pyjamas in there?" Aunt demanded, giving him her fierce look. He smiled like an angel and said the corner ripped when he was moving the parcel and he couldn't help but see.

Everyone burst out laughing, even you, Ben.

Then Aunt got her scribbled list out of her handbag and we began to fetch things we had hidden away. I am sorry, Ben, but I put your cloth ball into the box. Not your alphabet blocks though.

Father's Fifth-Form English class had taken up a collection and given him money for a Christmas turkey, so he donated that. We already had one turkey from Grandma and Grandy's farm. We will pack it all tomorrow and leave it on the family's doorstep on December 23 so the mother can stop worrying. They only live a few blocks away. Father put in a pair of socks Grandmother had knitted for him, and a pipe and tobacco. Then Aunt contributed a nightgown she had bought for herself to wear on Christmas. It was so pretty with lace at the neck and hem. Father took a good look at it and I'll bet he gets her one to take its place.

The oldest girl, Belinda, is twelve, so I gave her one of my precious books, *Eight Cousins.* I loved it when I was that age. I still love it, as a matter of fact.

Fanny says we should make the family some fudge. I felt my smile exactly matching hers. It was marvellous. She felt it too — I could see.

Wednesday, December 22, 1920

Dear Ben,

You took a step! And I was there to see you do it! You let go of the playpen railing and took a step to cut the corner and then you grabbed on with both fists to the other railing. You looked astonished at what you had just done. Then you sat down. I am watching to see you do it again.

You did!

When I ran to tell everyone, guess what? I caught

Fanny reading *Eight Cousins* with MY glasses on. I had left them on the table because they were pinching my nose. I could not believe that my sister, the one with the eagle eyes, was using my spectacles for reading.

I just stood staring. Then Aunt came in and stood beside me, both of us gazing at Fanny in amazement. "How would you like spectacles for Christmas, Francesca?" Aunt said softly.

Fanny went red as fire and dropped the book.

I had just remembered to tell about your first step when you let out a yell at being left alone so long, so I told them and they were most impressed. Then you did it again, which helped.

After supper

The Christmas boxes are all packed. That family will be so surprised to find their names on the parcels. Father made a card that read *With love and good wishes for a Merry Christmas from S. Claus.*

Theo stared at the card. Then he said, "You write just like Santa Claus." Father grinned and said he did his best.

Theo glared at him and shouted, "I'm still hanging up my stocking."

"Me too," said Father and gave him a giant hug.

Tomorrow night we are going to take the boxes

over after dark and leave them on that family's porch. Jo and Aunt will stay home with you, Ben, but the rest of us all want to go.

Thursday, December 23, 1920
Bedtime

Dear Ben,

We did it! It was incredibly exciting. There were two big boxes, one filled with food and one with presents. There was some tinsel too and Father slid in an envelope. I think it had some extra money in it for the family to spend any way they like. He put his finger to his lips so I did not ask.

We towed the boxes on our toboggan and stopped a couple of houses up the street. We hid behind a big clump of evergreens. Some places had wreaths on the door but theirs didn't. It was late and all the windows were dark.

Then Father took one of the boxes and Fan and I carried the other between us and Theo hopped and danced along, hoping we would drop something that he would have to rescue. We did. A box of popping corn. Theo scooped it up in a flash. We were *so* quiet, even though I had a terrible time not giggling. We put the boxes on their porch and skedaddled back to the toboggan. Father stayed behind long enough to knock on the door and then he ran after us. I have never seen him run so fast. We waited until a light went on and then we scurried away before they could come out. I wish we could have waited a couple of minutes more, just to see their faces.

Tomorrow night we will hang up our stockings, including yours, little Ben, and it will be lovely, but I don't think anything that happens from now on will be able to measure up to tonight.

Christmas Eve
December 24, 1920

Dear Ben,

Today we have all been busy getting the last-minute things ready and wrapping little secret treats to slide into stockings. You, the SMALLEST person, have the BIGGEST stocking because you have such a pile of gifts. It's big enough for a giant. Theo put out apples and carrots for the reindeer. Jo stayed at the hospital.

Aunt says we must go to bed. And I want to. It will make Christmas morning come faster. But it is hard to settle down. That is why I am writing to you.

Merry Christmas Eve, Benjamin.

Christmas Day
Saturday, December 25, 1920

Dear Ben,

Joy to the world! The Lord is come.

What a mixed-up, marvellous day! To think I was afraid it would be horrible. Theo woke us all up before it was light outside. He came for me and Fanny first and then we fetched you out of your crib. You were surprised to see us, but when we began to sing "Away in a Manger" you grinned and put up your arms to be lifted out. Then we got Aunt and Father and we were heading for the stairs when a sleepy voice called, "Wait for me, you lot!" Jo had come home in the night to be here to open her stocking. Carrie was with her and Jo had managed to hang up a stocking for her, which was perfect.

We all got silly things and nice things. I got a new book. I am always worried that Father and Aunt will forget I need a Christmas book — but they never have yet. It is *T. Tembarom* by Frances Hodgson Burnett. It is a grown-up love story! I have read almost half.

Right after we had our Christmas breakfast, Theo went out "to play in the snow." That was what he said. And then, Ben, you will never guess what he did. He went over to the street where we took the

Christmas boxes and started playing with the children there, and when he came home, he was jumping up and down with glee. He knew the whole story of how the family found the boxes. The mother even sent Belinda running over to tell her sister — the woman Aunt talked to — and the whole bunch of them got together and had a wonderful feast.

"That boy even liked the pyjamas," Theo told Aunt.

"They were the best pyjamas in the store," Aunt said.

Theo swore he did not even hint that he knew where the things had come from. He was so proud of himself for being such a detective.

I thought he was great until he pulled out his new play sword and started running around giving us all "the mark of Zorro." It is irritating. That sword does not cut but it sure bruises.

Connie came over at around two. She wanted Fan to come out for a walk. I held my breath, Ben, but Fan was as smooth as a queen. "I'm sorry," she said, "but we have company and Christmas is a family day. I'm busy tomorrow too. It's Ben's birthday and Margery James has invited me to go with her church group on a sleigh ride. I hope you have a merry Christmas." Then, while Connie was kind of hissing through her teeth, Fan quietly closed the door.

We read Dickens's *Christmas Carol* tonight. We started before supper so Theo would be able to stay up for it. But he fell asleep on the rug in front of the fireplace, leaning up against Hamlet.

Good night, Ben. You are almost a year old. This book will be finished tomorrow. I am going to miss writing to you.

But I got a lovely diary book, a fat one with big creamy pages, from Aunt for Christmas. Your clever mother always knows what I will be wanting.

Ben's First Birthday
Boxing Day, December 26, 1920

Dearest Ben,

You slept in! We were all waiting for you to wake us up early as usual and you didn't. Finally Theo began making a rumpus. He sang "Happy Birthday!" at the top of his voice and rushed about, stomping his feet, and at last you opened your eyes. And I was watching from the door and you saw me and you said, you actually said, "Fee." Then you said, "Fifi." But you can call me "Fifi" if you like, my sweet Ben.

Fan tried to get you to say "Fan," but you didn't. You didn't say "Fifi" again either, but never mind. I know you will.

You love your presents. And you walked another

step before you plunked down on your bottom. Such a clever child.

It was a lovely day from start to finish. Not one bit tangled. No frayed bits or ugly knots. I even told Fanny how jealous I had felt of Con when I began this book for you, and she gave me a tight hug.

People came to your birthday party, Ben. It seems strange to celebrate Jesus's birthday one day and yours the next. It is also strange to know that we will still be singing to the Little Lord Jesus when you are blowing out five candles, or ten, and you are not our "little lord Ben" any longer.

But you will have this Birthday Book to remind you of how we felt when you were almost one and I wrote this for you and learned to love you with all my heart.

Good night, little lord Ben. Goodbye, Ben's Book.
Love,
Fifi

Anya Soloniuk

Prisoners in the Promised Land
The Ukrainian Internment Diary of Anya Soloniuk
Spirit Lake, Quebec
April 13, 1914 – July 21, 1916

BY MARSHA FORCHUK SKRYPUCH

Anya's family was forced to spend part of World War I at Spirit Lake Internment Camp. They were regarded not only as foreigners but as "enemy aliens" who needed to be kept apart for Canada's security. Poverty still dogs them, even though Anya's factory job helps out.
Yet this Christmas promises to be happier than last year in the isolated internment camp . . . if old resentments can be laid to rest.

An Unexpected Visitor

Monday, December 18, 1916

Dear Irena,

My supervisor gave me a few sheets from his ledger book, so I can finally write to you and let you know everything that's been happening to me. I will keep these pages with me, and once I have filled them all I will mail them. Postage is so dear, after all. Write back when you are able. You are in my heart.

I think the supervisor feels sorry for me because I am sitting by myself at lunch yet again. Now that I am promoted, the other girls make strange with me. I don't mean Slava or Maureen. But since my promotion, we three no longer have lunch at the same time.

We have this huge order of infantry uniforms and it makes my head ache. The material is coarser than the ladies' blouses we usually sew, and the girls are not used to it. I cringe each time a needle pierces their fingertips. Only weeks ago, it was me at one of those machines.

As sad as I am for the girls, I cannot help but think of what these uniforms are being used for. So many people are still being sent across the ocean to fight in this terrible war. And what of our old country, Irena? I know that fighting is going on right in Ukraine. Will a Canadian soldier wearing one of these uniforms end up fighting my old neighbours in Horoshova?

The whistle has sounded. Must get back to work.

Before bed

Oy, Irena! Stefan showed me the coins he earned today! He sold all the scarves and every pair of mittens.

I am relieved. The last weeks had not been going well for Stefan's new business, but with Christmas near, it is picking up. He saves every penny he can.

It is so crowded in our flat with Baba, Mama, Tato and Mykola, of course, but add to that, Slava (will her father ever come home?) and Stefan, plus his mother and father. When his older brothers come home from the war, we'll be in a pickle. Where could they possibly sleep? At least with all these people, it's nice and warm even on the coldest nights.

Speaking of Stefan's brothers, he got a Christmas card from Ivan — that's the brother who calls himself John Pember. He is fighting in France. He decorated the card by stitching in patterns and words with red and green thread. He wrote in his regiment motto, *Facta non verba,* and also, *Merry Christmas.*

I do not know what *Facta non verba* means.

Tomorrow is St. Nicholas Day. I can hardly wait! I have special gifts for everyone.

Tuesday, December 19, 1916
St. Nicholas Day

Mama asked Mrs. Haggarty. *Facta non verba* is Latin for "Actions, not words." I like that motto, don't you?

Oh, Irena, Stefan has given me the most interesting gift. I cannot imagine how

Wednesday, December 20, 1916

I'm sorry, Irena. I had to end suddenly last night. It is difficult to find a time or place to write when I am at home. Once the mattresses are rolled out and the sheet strung across the middle of the room, I can barely move! The worst is when someone has to get up in the middle of the night to go to the outhouse. Stefan's mother tripped on my foot last night and almost fell on top of Baba.

Tato blew the lights out just as I was about to write down details of Stefan's gift. It is just a small envelope with my name written on the front in neat script, in green ink. Inside is a flat card that says this:

You are cordially invited
to Afternoon Tea
with
Mister Stefan Pemlych
at
The Restaurant
at
Ogilvy's Department Store
on
Saturday, December 30, 1916
at
4 o'clock

I could tell that Stefan wrote it himself, but it must have taken him a long time because penmanship is not his strength.

Do you know what "Afternoon Tea" is, Irena? I thought it was a cup of tea in the afternoon, but Stefan says I am wrong — it does include tea but it isn't what I think. Stefan just grins when I try to get him to tell me more. I can hardly wait until December 30!

Thursday, December 21, 1916

Irena, when I was coming home from work yesterday, I saw a man who must have once been a soldier. He was standing at the corner of a building, with his collar turned up against the cold. There was something familiar about the way he held himself. Don't ask me why, but I knew he had been in the army even though he wasn't wearing a uniform. He looked cold and lonely, and he was holding out his cap, begging for money. I walked quickly by without looking up. I had no money to give.

Oy, Irena, do you think I'm a bad person for walking so quickly away?

Friday, December 22, 1916

Dear Irena,

I am sitting here at work even though I should have left for home an hour ago. I keep on looking up at the windows and wondering how I will ever get home. The snowflakes are so thick and furious that I cannot see anything but white. The wind is so strong and damp that I can feel it in my bones. The supervisor let us stay inside because he was afraid we would get lost if we tried to get home. Maybe I will have to stay here all night. It is so dark outside.

Saturday, December 23, 1916

Oy, Irena, what a time we've been having. I am safe at home right now and it is early afternoon. Just as I was writing to you yesterday, the door to the factory opened up. A swirl of wind and sleet came through and with it, Tato and Stefan. When they saw that

Slava and I weren't at home, they came to get us.

By the time we got to our flat, I was soaked through and shivering. Slava slipped on a patch of ice and nearly turned her ankle.

It was much colder when we walked to work this morning, but I prefer cold to wet. The air was crisp and fresh and there was no wind. The snow sparkled like jewels in the sun. I love it when we have a snow-fall. The streets look so clean.

Sunday, December 24, 1916

When Mama came home from work yesterday, she had a giant raw turkey. She said that Mrs. Haggarty gave each of the kitchen staff a turkey to take home for Canadian Christmas dinner. Wasn't that nice of her? Have you ever eaten turkey? I haven't. Mama has packed it in snow to keep it cold and Baba is going to roast it tomorrow.

Monday December 25, 1916
Five days before Afternoon Tea with Stefan!

Dear Irena,

I am writing to you from home even though it is the middle of the day and a Monday. Today is Canadian Christmas, so we had a day off work. My stomach is grumbling. All I can smell is the aroma of roasting turkey. Baba stuffed it with bread and rubbed the outside with garlic and pepper and it has been roasting ever since. Mama says that no one at Mrs. Haggarty's household ever uses garlic. How can someone not like garlic?

I can hardly wait to try this turkey. Mrs. Pemlych has made a compote with cranberries just like in the old country. She says that Canadians eat this with their turkey. Imagine eating sweets with meat! Canadians have some interesting customs, and I want to try all of them. I love that we get to celebrate Canadian Christmas and real Christmas. Are you celebrating both Christmases too, Irena?

P.S.
Oy, Irena. I think I could burst. Turkey is tasty, especially the dark meat. Cranberry compote is heavenly with it.

Tuesday, December 26, 1916
Four days before Afternoon Tea with Stefan!

Dear Irena,

In the newspaper today there is a photograph of a mountain of potatoes. People in Belgium are starving, and these potatoes are for them. I feel so guilty. Here I am, still full of turkey, when across the ocean people have nothing. If Belgians are starving, what is it like in our old country? They must be starving too. I wish I could wrap up some of our turkey and send it to Horoshova.

There is also a story about Santa Claus visiting wounded Canadian soldiers in Britain. Don't you think Santa Claus is an interesting name for St. Nicholas? These soldiers were wounded in France. I wonder if John Pember is one of them? I hope not. Do you know what the soldiers got? Turkey! I hope they got cranberry compote too!

Wednesday, December 27, 1916
Three days before Afternoon Tea with Stefan!

In the paper today was a list of Canadian soldiers who have been killed. It makes me so sad to think of this terrible war and everyone who suffers — on both sides.

Thursday, December 28, 1916

Dear Irena,

I saw that man again, and you will never believe this. He is Howard Smythe, that awful guard from the internment camp! No wonder he looked familiar. He was huddled at the same street corner, his arms crossed in front of him. It was mild today, with just a little bit of new snow, yet Howard Smythe was shivering as if he had been standing in the street for a very long time. Is he no longer a guard at Kapuskasing Internment Camp? I wonder where he works and where he lives.

Friday, December 29, 1916
Afternoon Tea tomorrow with Stefan!

Oy, Irena. It is midnight, yet I just got home from work. I have moved a chair to the window and opened the curtain just a bit so I can write by the light of the street lamp. The supervisor wanted to get the uniforms finished before the end of the month because he's expecting another big order in January. He offered a bonus to anyone who would stay late. There were only a few of us who agreed to stay, and that included Slava, Maureen and me. He sent a messenger home to our families so they wouldn't worry, and then we worked straight through the evening. At nine o'clock he brought in fish and chips wrapped in newspaper and he also gave us each a glass bottle of a drink called Coca Cola. The Coca Cola bubbles up on my tongue in a most delightful way. I was uneasy about eating food from a newspaper, but the supervisor said that this was a very popular dish with Canadians. The fish had a lovely crispy coating just like Baba makes and what is called "chips" is actually much like our own *smazhena kartoflia,* so you can imagine how delicious it is. We kept on sewing and finished the order just after 11 p.m. The supervisor took us home in his sleigh and he paid us 25¢ each. That is in addition to the 30¢ I would have made today anyway. I am exhausted and my hands ache but I cannot sleep. I am so looking forward to tomorrow.

Saturday December 30, 1916

Dear Irena,

Finally, it's the day of our Afternoon Tea!

As soon as the factory closed at noon, I walked home quickly. I dressed in my best Sunday skirt and blouse and Stefan put on the good white shirt I made him for St. Nicholas Day. It was bitterly cold so we bundled warmly and took the trolley downtown. *Oy,* Irena! In all the time we have lived here, I have never been in one of those fancy stores in downtown Montreal.

Ogilvy's has giant glass display cases filled with items for ladies, like perfumes and gloves and hats. As we wandered through, I was dizzy with the variety. And there is an elevator, Irena. We stepped inside and a man in a uniform asked us to step to the back. My heart fluttered as he closed the door with the big lever. It was like being on that crowded ship again. Suddenly, the floor moved! We took the elevator to the very top, which is where the Ogilvy's Restaurant is. Irena, you will never guess what happened next! A man wearing a short skirt greeted us, took our coats, and led us to a table. I hardly knew where to look. He was wearing long woollen socks but his knees were bare. My face felt hot with embarrassment, but Stefan just grinned at me. He said that the man was wearing a kilt, which is the tradition for men from Scotland. Ogilvy's is a Scottish store, Irena. His kilt was in green, black and red "tartan plaid," which is a very pretty pattern. The cloths covering the tables had the same pattern. Once we were seated, I looked around and was glad that I had worn my Sunday best. Mostly the tables were taken up by older ladies and they were all well-dressed. A woman at a table not far from ours looked us up and down when she thought I wasn't looking. I don't think that was very nice of her. Her clothing might be more expensive than ours, and she may have fancy hair, but I think our manners are better!

A lady in a long (thank goodness!) plaid skirt came over and gave a menu to Stefan. He looked at it as if he knew what he was doing, then told her that we would both like the "high tea."

A few minutes later, she came back and placed a tray on our table. On it was a flowered porcelain teapot, two dainty teacups, cream, milk, sugar, lemon and spoons. This puzzled me. Stefan had said that it was NOT just tea, but that's what it looked like. As we let it steep, the lady came back. She placed a three-tiered tray beside the tea service. *Oy*, Irena, you should have seen what it held. On the bottom tier were delicate bite-sized sandwiches on white bread. Here are the different kinds — strawberry jam with butter, cucumber, salmon, egg, ham and cheese. On the middle tier were different biscuits. There were raisin scones, crispy buns and English muffins. On the top tier were what she called *petit fours* — beautiful little cakes that look like pastel Christmas presents. I think it must be called a high tea because the plate is so tall.

We ate and chatted for over an hour but we never did get to the bottom of the teapot. The lady kept filling it back up with boiling water. There were still some sandwiches and *petit fours* on the plate when we were finished, so the lady put them in a small box for us to take home. We walked through the rest of the store and then we went outside to wait for the trolley.

As the cold air hit my face, I thought of the people across the ocean with not enough food, and of all the soldiers who were fighting in this terrible war. All at once, the dainty sandwiches, buns and sweets felt heavy on my stomach. I looked at the box that I held in my hands, then said to Stefan, "There is someone I know who is hungry."

We caught the trolley but got off a few stops before our flat. I explained to Stefan who I was looking for. *Oy*,

Irena! Stefan's face went white with anger. "After all that he did to us, you're going to feed *him?*" he asked.

It was our first argument in a long time. In the end, Stefan was still not happy with my decision, but he agreed to come with me to "protect" me. We walked to where Howard Smythe usually stood, but he wasn't there. So I left the small box on a ledge, hoping he would see it when he came back.

Monday, January 1, 1917

In the paper today was a story about an internment camp in Sudbury that caught on fire. One man died and many others had to flee. Reading that story brought back bad memories, Irena. And on the way to work today, I saw Howard Smythe again. He looked right at me and I looked back, but neither of us said a word or even nodded like we knew each other. I hope he found the food that I left him. Irena, will you think I am terrible if I admit to you that — even though he is in a bad way now — every time I see him, I still get angry about what happened to us at the camp?

Wednesday, January 3, 1917

The same group of us worked after hours at the factory on Tuesday. The supervisor brought us fish and chips again and that lovely Coca Cola. Why is it that when I work late, I have trouble sleeping? You would think that I would be extra tired.

Howard Smythe was standing in his usual place when I walked to work this morning, and this time he said something. I'm not sure what he said because of the wind. I had a feeling of being followed on the way home from work. I kept on turning, but saw no one. Perhaps it is all in my mind.

Friday, January 5, 1917

Oy, Irena, now I am frightened. When I left for work yesterday morning, I saw Howard Smythe again. He wasn't in his usual spot. Instead, he was leaning against the building right across the road from our flat. Why was he doing that?

Today I didn't see Howard Smythe at all. I did tell Tato, and he and Stefan and Mr. Pemlych walked all over our neighbourhood in the pouring rain this evening looking for him. Why is it that I am more troubled by his disappearance than by his watching us? Tomorrow is *Svyat Vechir*, and I should be looking forward to it, but instead I am brooding.

Saturday, January 6, 1917
Svyat Vechir

Dear Irena,

As I walked home from work this morning, I was thinking about all that I have seen and done since last

Ukrainian Christmas Eve. We are no longer at the internment camp, and that is a relief. I am making good money at the factory, and so is Tato at his factory. Mama's job with Mrs. Haggarty is secure. Mykola is able to go to school again. Am I awful to admit that I am jealous of my little brother? How I long to go back to school myself. But I know that when the war ends, we all may be out of work yet again. We must save our money while we can. Although it is crowded in our tiny flat, I like living close to Stefan and his family. It makes me feel safe. I am happy, Irena. I truly am. There is just one nagging problem, and that is Howard Smythe.

Sunday, January 7, 1917
Rizdvo

Dear Irena,

I have so much to tell you, yet so little paper left.

Last night Mykola was perched by the window, waiting for the first star so we could begin our meal. Suddenly he cried, "A man is out there, staring at me."

It was Howard Smythe!

Tato put on his coat and stepped outside. From inside, all we could hear were muffled sounds. Have you been to a silent movie, Irena? I haven't, but I think going to one must be like watching Tato and Howard Smythe through the window. Mr. Pemlych and Stefan wanted to go out too, but Mama blocked the door, saying it looked under control. They argued like what seemed forever, but then all at once it seemed over. Tato held out his hand and Howard Smythe shook it. Then the door opened, and both walked in.

Howard Smythe removed his coat and hat and stood in the threshold. The clothes he had on under the coat were shabby and not exactly clean and he seemed embarrassed about that.

Tato led Howard Smythe to our table and said, "We are honoured to have you join us this evening."

I was shocked speechless, Irena. Yes, it was *Svyat Vechir*, and of course it is traditional to invite strangers to share our meal on this night — but *Howard Smythe*? What had he and Tato talked about out there?

At first, conversation was awkward and polite, but then Mykola blurted out, "Aren't you that soldier who was so mean to Anya at the internment camp?"

Tato gave Mykola a thunderous look and I could feel the heat in my face. Howard Smythe blinked and set down his fork. "You are right, son," he said.

Then he turned to me. "I am sorry for what I did to you," he told me.

I was so shocked, Irena, that I just nodded.

Howard Smythe sighed and then his story poured

out. He was dishonourably discharged from the army several weeks ago and moved back to Montreal. He cannot get a job because of his dishonourable discharge and he has been living at the YMCA and begging in the streets.

"I know now that is was hard for you when you came to this country," he said. "Back then, I just thought of you all as dirty foreigners."

I gasped when he said that, Irena. Mama went still.

"When I came back here and saw that you had a job when I couldn't get one, that made me angry." He shook his head, then looked me in the eye. "I saw you leave that box of food for me," he said. "It made me reconsider." Then he said, "I wanted to thank you for your kindness."

Oy, Irena! It was such an amazing evening. I feel like I have had a thorn taken out of my heart. After dinner was over and Howard Smythe had gone home, I perched on Tato's knee, just like I used to when I was younger.

"For what do I owe this honour?" asked Tato.

"I want to thank you for inviting Howard Smythe to dinner."

Tato hugged me and said, "It was *Svyat Vechir*. And yes, it does feel good to let go of the anger."

"I wish there was something else we could do for him."

"I'm thinking the same thing," said Tato. "We need help at the factory. If I say something nice about him, and Mr. Pemlych does the same, perhaps Howard Smythe can get a job there."

Words cannot express how good this makes me feel, Irena. I hope Tato's plan works. It reminds me of John Pember's motto: *Actions, not words.*

I have run out of paper, so I will stop here. Stefan and I are going to take a walk in the snow. The world outside looks like fresh paper. I have turned over a dark chapter in my life and I am anxious for a fresh start.

I hope you like the red ribbon I used to tie all of these pages together with. I bought it at an after-Christmas sale. It should look lovely in your hair.

Please write soon, dear Irena. I will write again when I get more paper.

As always, your friend,
Anya

Devorah Bernstein

Turned Away
The World War II Diary of Devorah Bernstein
Winnipeg, Manitoba
December 6, 1941 – November 5, 1942

By Carol Matas

Devorah is still trying to make others aware of the desperate plight of Jews in Europe under Hitler's Nazi regime. And she's still worried about her brothers overseas, one a pilot with the RAF, one in a Japanese POW camp. A forced visit with her no-nonsense Zionist grandmother, and helping out a neighbour who has lost two sons to the War, give Dev a different take on what really makes a difference in people's lives.

Something That Matters

Monday, December 6, 1943

Murder!!!

Murder, Dear Diary. It's like something out of one of my Agatha Christie novels. A young waitress murdered at the Marlborough Hotel. Her body was found by her parents at 4:40 a.m. She'd been strangled!!

Mommy actually tried to hide the newspaper from me, worried it would upset me. Of course I feel terrible for this girl. But what was the story behind it? What could have happened? If only I were like Miss Marple or Hercule Poirot, I could waltz down there and have the whole mystery solved in no time.

It's all we could talk about after school at our first carolling practice. Elizabeth is organizing all of us on our street — Paul, me and Laura. I'm happy about that because I love Christmas carols. Especially "Silent Night " and "We Three Kings of Orient Are." We hardly got any practising done, though, because we were all wondering if we are in danger now and if this murderer is wandering around Winnipeg and if we should sleep with a knife, or at the very least lock our windows and doors! The paper says the girl was in love with a tall, dark, handsome older man — a stranger until recently. I'll certainly keep my eyes peeled for anyone like that.

Thursday, December 9, 1943

Today's paper says that a mysterious man approached another girl and promised her a job in Vancouver, but she turned him down. It's thought that he is the same older fellow who promised the other girl, the strangled one, a job too! This other girl said she's afraid that she is next on his list!! He doesn't sound like the type of criminal who sneaks into people's houses — no, he plans and probably picks a pretty girl, and then entices her.

Later

A letter from Adam!!
And one just for me.

Dearest Dev,

I can't tell you much of anything, little sister, because the censors will just black it out anyway, but you read the papers and can see how well the Italian campaign is going for the troops there. Things are definitely looking up! Outside of the day-to-day living, which is getting worse and worse. I dream of scrambled eggs and corned beef sandwiches and pickles! Not the canned kind you get here but Aunt Adele's, all crispy and full of garlic. Mom's packages are so wonderful — we look forward to them and also to the little things you add. Oh, how I love the Mars toasted almond bars you send.

Keep up your good work with the TO's. I think it's a great name your group chose — I remember when you were eight and I was explaining the concept of Tikkun Olam to you. Do you remember me telling you that it means "to heal the world" and you asked me if there was a Band-Aid big enough for that? Well, the world certainly needs help! I'm glad your group is educating both kids and adults about the refugees and how Canada won't take any Jews.

Maybe the more people learn, the more they'll complain to the government and pressure them to change their mind. Although, Devvy, I wonder if it's already too late. We hear such horrors over here — that the Jews who have been rounded up are being methodically murdered.

By the time the Canadian government changes its tune, it will probably be too late for the Jews of

Europe. But that doesn't mean you should give up. All you can do is keep trying.

Give my love to Mom and Dad, and remember to study hard for your exams coming up!

Your older (and wiser) brother,
Adam

Oh how I miss him. I can't help but remember his last visit when he took me up in the air for my first-ever flight. Adam and his fellow fliers are the bravest men in the entire world, that's certain.

Friday, December 10, 1943

Shoes!! Apparently the murder victim bought a pair of shoes but someone RETURNED them later that day for two pairs of a smaller size!! For his next victim? He wanted to give them as a present to the next girl, I'll bet, to get in her good books. Oh, very devious.

Saturday, December 11, 1943
Shabbat

What a busy day. I met the TO's downtown for a movie, although we had an awful fight about which one to see. Marcie wanted to see *A Lady Takes a Chance* because Jean Arthur is in it and we all love her. Ruthie wanted to see *Lassie Come Home*, but

David said it was too babyish for us. I wanted to sneak into *Dead Men Walk* and *Ghost and the Guest* — the ad won't show any pictures because it would be too scary!! Finally we all agreed on *Lassie,* and I must admit it was pretty good and had us crying, even though Roddy McDowall is quite the ham. But Lassie is amazing. I swear that dog is smarter than half the kids in my class!

After that we went shopping for presents for friends who celebrate Christmas. I needed something for Elizabeth. I got her Devon Violets cologne for 50¢. I know she loves anything with violets. Ruthie bought her younger brother a birthday present, a cardboard Noah's Ark for 98¢. I think he'll destroy it in minutes, but she thought it was adorable.

We went to The Chocolate Shop afterward and talked about what we could do for the next few weeks. We agreed that, at our school concerts, we should each try to give a talk about the refugees, if we are allowed. So I'll ask if I can speak at ours for a few minutes.

Now I'm going to read my new book, *Poirot Investigates.*

Tuesday, December 14, 1943

They caught him!!
The murderer.
He is 42 and lived in the same boarding house on

Spence Street where the poor victim lived. She was just 16! And he was the one who called the police and who "found" her body! And he isn't tall and dark — he's small, with grey hair. Reality is much less thrilling than the picture the paper painted, that's for sure.

Thursday, December 16, 1943

Churchill is very sick — with pneumonia!

Friday, December 17, 1943

Churchill is improving. What a relief! Without him to lead the Allies, Hitler might still find a way to win. Who knows?

Later

Today was the last day of school, and the day of the concert. I haven't written to you every day this week, Diary, because I've been preparing my speech, as well as studying and writing my exams.

I was given only 2 minutes for my speech! Two minutes to tell everyone about what's going on with Jews over there and how Canada is pretending nothing is happening and how they refuse to help.

Daddy helped me with it. He wanted me to take some things out, but I wouldn't. Here's my speech. I've written it out for posterity:

Thank you to Principal Lester for the opportunity to give this talk.

Teachers, parents, and fellow students, I speak to you today about an issue that you are probably familiar with in some ways, but in other ways, you might not know the entire story. We are very proud of our country and how we are fighting the Nazis and I have two brothers overseas, one with the RAF and one with the Winnipeg Grenadiers who's now a POW. But I also have family in France and we have been trying to get them over here ever since 1941, but we can't! (At this point I almost burst into tears and had to stop for a moment and catch my breath.)

The Canadian government doesn't want Jewish refugees. The men in charge don't like Jews. (At this point some people gasped and others made disapproving noises, but most, I think, were upset with *me* for saying it out loud, not upset with the *government* for doing it.) But I know that most people in Canada don't feel that way. (Well, I certainly hope not.) And so I ask for all of you to write the person in charge, Mr. Blair, and ask him — no, *demand* — that he open up our country to any refugees who can still escape. The truth is, there aren't too many anymore, but if some manage to get to Spain or other countries, then let them come here. Only a year ago there were thousands of children in France who had visas to come to Canada, but the door was shut to them and now they might be dead. We must try to save anyone we can — even one child is important!

Thank you for your time and for your consideration. (That was Daddy's addition.)

There was polite applause, but I can't say it was a big hit. Still, I'm glad I did it, although it felt funny standing up as a Jew. I felt that everyone might look at me differently . . . but I can't help that. It's nothing compared to what the Jews in Europe are going through, is it?

Saturday, December 18, 1943

Baba Tema has fallen and broken her foot and sprained her wrist! And Mommy has offered me as her helper for the holidays. So no carolling with my friends. I'm to be shipped off to the North End to spend 2 whole weeks with a woman who's never said a nice word to me in my life. And who scares me! I've cried, I've screamed, I've tried reasoning, everything — nothing helped. Mommy is unwavering. She is busy with a Christmas push to get special packages to the troops and says that's far more important than my holidays. (And she doesn't understand why carolling is so important to me anyway — especially since we're Jewish! I tried to explain that I love the songs and that it's fun, but she really doesn't think it's worth a thought, considering Baba needs me.)

Sunday, December 19, 1943

Today was my first day with Baba Tema. What a disaster! I was going to have so much fun this holiday. I can't even see Marcie because Baba doesn't want my friends over — they are too noisy, apparently. PLUS, she has a neighbour right next door who also needs help and Baba is sending me over there to help *her* out as well — if there should be any precious minutes when she won't be working me until I drop!! Things are going from bad to worse. At least the whole family was here for dinner tonight, so I won't be alone with Baba until tomorrow.

Monday, December 20, 1943

War news is excellent. General Montgomery's army overran enemy positions in Italy and so did U.S. troops. We're winning, we're winning, we're winning! Oh, and tomorrow is the first night of Chanukah, so the family will all be back then, thank goodness.

Baba made me eat oatmeal for breakfast and said I should be happy for it. I don't mind it if it's covered in sugar and milk, but with no sugar and made with water, it's disgusting. And to top it off, I had to cook it! For both of us.

Night

After breakfast Baba quizzed me about what I knew about Palestine and apparently it isn't enough, because she made me sit for an hour at the kitchen table while she watched me with an evil eye as I read a book on Palestine and Zionism. I told her I understand that we want and need our own Jewish homeland, but that wasn't enough for her. And then she made me read aloud from a newspaper article on Hadassah and what they do. And then she had me shovel the walk and her neighbour's walk, and then make lunch — herring!!! Herring, ugh, double ugh. And then she had me clean up and study some more, and write letters for her to all these politicians and even to people in Britain. She seems to be very important. I wonder if you need to be tough as nails like she is to be important.

Tuesday, December 21, 1943

I don't even know where to start!

Baba has banned *Peril at End House*, the Agatha Christie novel I'm right in the middle of! She says that my obsession with made-up murder and mayhem is unhealthy. Unhealthy! I might have mentioned the waitress murder a few times, just to make conversation, because sitting in silence with Baba is so uncomfortable, as well as being boring. She doesn't like to "chit chat," as she says. And she says that if I'm reading, it should be something worthwhile, like a history book, and she's given me the history of England with a special emphasis on the British Mandate, Palestine. How do you read *that* when it's night and you're snuggled up under the covers?

Night

Adam was one of the fliers involved in a huge raid over France that downed seven Nazi planes! It's in the paper today! And I'm not even at school so I can boast about him. The Allies dropped 2000 tons of explosives on Frankfurt yesterday too.

I complained bitterly to Mommy and Daddy when they were here tonight for the Chanukah party. But Mommy is working till midnight every night packing boxes for the troops, and Daddy is treating an entire group of fliers in from the base at Gimli and is also overwhelmed, so it seems I'm on my own. The party was so subdued, with just me as the only child there getting presents.

We lit the first candle on the Menorah, and Daddy retold the story of the Chanukah lights, just as he does every Chanukah: how the Maccabees had fought Antiochus, and won, but there was only enough oil to keep the eternal flame in the Temple burning for one day, yet the flame burned for eight days and that was the miracle. He added that we would beat Hitler too. And then Baba said, "Bah," or "Pshaw," or something like that, and added that Chanukah had really been a civil war between the traditional Jews and those that had been assimilated into the Syrian culture and were praying to Zeus. I barely listened, because this same fight between Baba and Daddy happens every year.

I was given a little chocolate and some Chanukah *gelt* and that was it. Daddy almost fell asleep after dinner.

Wednesday, December 22, 1943

I spent this morning reading the history book out loud to Baba, as she is not convinced that I am actually reading it on my own. When I finished the chapter on the Arab riots of 1921, she said, "Is that enough murder and mayhem for you?" Before I could answer she had me fix our lunch, and then as soon as I'd washed up she sent me next door to spend the entire afternoon with Mrs. Norman. Mrs. Norman is an older woman, not as old as Baba but lots older than Mommy. She needed help making a scrapbook. She has bad arthritis in her hands and can't glue or cut anything. Her dining room table was covered in newspapers — articles about the war and about certain regiments and certain battles. She told me that she wanted everything sorted into three piles. There was to be a pile for each son. And then she said to me, "Of course, two of them are dead. One at sea, one in the Battle of Britain. The third is in Japan with the Winnipeg Grenadiers and we don't know what has happened to him."

I told her that my brother Morris is also there and that we had had news that he was alive. So had she, about her son Matthew, but she said she had no faith that the Japanese would keep him alive to the end of the war.

I felt so sorry for her. Two sons dead, and a third, who knows? And then she told me that her husband, who had been in poor health, died of a heart attack after finding out about his second son.

I can't even understand how Mrs. Norman is still alive. I think I would have died of grief like her husband. She must have seen that in my face because she said, "The boys are alive in here" — at that she put her hand over her heart — "and so is my dear Paul. If I die then they really will be dead, with no one to keep their memory alive. That's why I'm trying to make these scrapbooks, but my hands won't co-operate."

So I told her that I'd be happy to help and immediately got down to work, partly because I didn't know how or what to say to her. Most of the articles were marked with a pen, although they still needed to be clipped, and then put in order by dates and times. She had lots of family pictures as well and wanted them interspersed with the stories from the *Free Press* and sometimes *The Globe and Mail* and even some papers from London, England, that she had managed to get.

As I sorted and picked out an article she would talk about the attack or the operation and what she had heard about it from her sons, as opposed to what the papers had said. Of course, her sons couldn't write too much because of the censors, but when they came home on leave she heard quite a few stories. I suggested that we should write those down and put them in the scrapbook too. So she told me the story and I printed it out on a piece of foolscap and then we pasted that in as well. It was dinnertime before I knew it and we had only gotten a quarter way through the first scrapbook.

I said goodbye and hurried back to Baba's to make her dinner. She asked me how the afternoon was. I told her how sorry I felt for Mrs. Norman. She just nodded and didn't say anything and I couldn't tell what she was thinking.

Thursday, December 23, 1943

I spent the morning cleaning Baba's house and then writing more letters for her. They are odd letters and I don't understand most of them, and when I ask Baba she just tells me to write what she dictates. It's almost like she is writing in code. I know this sounds crazy, but I've started to wonder if Baba is a spy. She keeps writing letters about buying hammers and nuts and bolts and where they should be delivered and how. What does Baba have to do with nuts and bolts and hammers? She has told me that we must work to make Palestine a homeland for any Jews who manage to survive, but she says that won't happen without a fight. All right, Diary, here's what I'm thinking. Could hammers be code for GUNS? Now I'm *really* scared of Baba!!!

I spent this afternoon with Mrs. Norman again. We managed to get one complete scrapbook done. Baba had told me to invite her for dinner and so we both went over to Baba's and showed her the scrapbook. For a moment Baba looked like she might almost smile. I mean, I think I saw the corner of her mouth turn up just a little.

I made noodles and cut some onions up and fried them and mixed them into the noodles with a little cheese and Mrs. Norman said it was very good. Baba just grunted.

When I woke up this morning Baba said that if I wanted I could go back to the South End and do my carolling with my friends tonight. Daddy says he misses me and he'll come pick me up around 3. I jumped up and down and screamed, I was so happy. And then when I'd gone quiet, she said, "Of course you'll have to disappoint Mrs. Norman, who still needs help with her project." And then she stared at me and didn't say anything more.

Well, I wasn't going to let her ruin my fun by some stupid stares. I hadn't seen my friends in days and I'd been working hard and I deserved to go!

I cooked Baba lunch and then I wrote more letters for her and waited impatiently for Daddy to arrive. I was so happy to see him.

"Christmas Eve!" he said "And it looks like it'll be a beautiful night. Mild weather and a light snow — perfect for carolling." He turned to Baba. "You must have been happy to have Devorah here," he said to her.

She looked straight at me and said, "Happiness can mean very different things to different people. And it can come in many different forms."

Daddy laughed. He never takes Baba very seriously. "Oh, Mama," he said, "everything doesn't need to be a lesson."

She raised her eyebrows as if she didn't agree with that.

I put on my coat and we went out to the car. As Daddy started driving, I asked him what Baba had meant. He thought for a moment and then said, "I suppose she means that happiness and fun can be two different things. You want to have fun tonight. She doesn't put much store in fun. But I think you *should* have fun."

"She won't even let me read my murder mysteries," I told him. "She's against fun altogether!"

And yet, something was nagging at me.

I kept thinking about Mrs. Norman, all alone in her house on Christmas Eve, with no husband, two sons dead and one missing, and then I'd get mad and try to stop thinking about her, and finally Daddy said, "You're muttering and shaking your head." And that's when I sighed and asked him to take me back to Baba's house. He laughed, thinking I was joking, but I wasn't. So he turned the car around and as we drove back there I told him about Mrs. Norman and the scrapbooks. When we got there he gave me a big hug and I could see he had tears in his eyes! I asked him what was wrong and he said "Nothing," but before I got out of the car he told me he thought I was growing up very fast.

When I entered Baba's house she was trying to put

some water on the stove to boil, but she couldn't manage, so I helped her and she told me that we should ask Mrs. Norman over again. She didn't seem at all happy to see me, but that's no surprise. When I went to Mrs. Norman's to invite her over she was so happy she hugged me! We worked on the scrapbooks until suppertime and then we went over to Baba's and she had already put a brisket in the oven so I made potatoes and she made some turnips to mix in with them and we had quite a delicious dinner. AND we had wine. Mine was mixed with water — but still! In fact I'm feeling a little tipsy as I write this.

Monday, December 27, 1943

Well, this will go down as the strangest holiday ever, that's for sure. I spent all of Christmas Day with Mrs. Norman, plus the last two afternoons, and we finished the scrapbooks! She was so happy!

And when I went to Baba's to make dinner she told me I could have my Agatha Christie book back. I asked why. She said because I enjoyed them and that was all right, but that I should try to remember that there were real people being murdered every day by the Nazis, especially Jews, and that we should pay attention to the real world. And then she said, "Those boys next door were murdered. In war, true, but by Nazi thugs, or by people obeying the orders of Nazi thugs."

And tonight as I get ready to go home I realize that although this hasn't been "fun," I've maybe had the best holidays ever. I can't describe it exactly, except to say that it's like a good feeling inside. I did something that matters, and that makes me feel happy. And although Baba never ever seems to have fun, she really feels that what she is doing is important, and maybe that makes *her* happy.

I wonder if she really is a spy.

GENEVIÈVE AUBUCHON

THE DEATH OF MY COUNTRY

THE PLAINS OF ABRAHAM DIARY
OF GENEVIÈVE AUBUCHON
QUÉBEC, NEW FRANCE

LE 8 AVRIL 1759 – LE 1ᴱᴿ JANVIER 1760

BY MAXINE TROTTIER

*Geneviève feared for her brother's life when he
and his friend fought to defend New France against
the British siege of their city. Their hopes came undone
in one day following a fierce battle on the Plains
of Abraham. With Québec in British hands, everything
— everything — changed. And now another shift
in their fortunes brings a new challenge.*

These Three Gifts

Montréal. I can scarcely believe that we have arrived. I worried that I would not be able to sleep in Monsieur Bélanger's house, which is a house of death, but the weariness of two days travel has overcome my fears.

Tomorrow Madame Claire's uncle will be buried in Notre Dame Basilica.

It is over. Monsieur Bélanger has been laid to rest. It would be best, though, to set down exactly what has happened. Andrew believes that a journal should be a clear picture of events, like a straight road. It comes from being an officer, I suppose. I am not an officer, and so I fear that my journal is often like a crooked path. As a good friend, Andrew understands this. Mère Esther says it is because of my Abenaki blood, that it is my nature to take a different route, but that it is of no consequence. The important thing is arriving.

So. Three days ago, Mme Claire received shocking news by way of a letter from a Montréal lawyer, one Monsieur Verges. Her ancient uncle, M. Balthazar Bélanger, had passed away suddenly, apparently from an apoplexy. The funeral would be on the coming Tuesday if Mme Claire wished to attend. She did, and so immediately made plans to journey. I had never met the deceased man, and so I felt no sadness, I must admit. I did feel a bit of excitement, though, since I had never seen Montréal.

There was no time then to write about any of that. Governor Murray arranged for a carriage upon hearing the news. The governor, although he is British, is a considerate man. When Mme refused a military escort, Governor Murray insisted that Chegual travel with us, which pleased me, since I can never get enough of my brother's company. Cook said that she would look after Wigwedi and La Bave, but that they had best not get into mischief. Wigwedi, in spite of having only three legs, can jump remarkably high, even for a rabbit, and is sometimes guilty of stealing vegetables from Cook's table. La Bave's only crime is drooling, but Cook does not care for dog drool on her clean floors.

The journey was as pleasant as could be expected. Still, I wish there had been more snow, so as to hide the remains of farmhouses that the British burned last year. To see Québec itself in ruins is bad enough. It bothered me somehow, when we arrived, to note how little damage was done to Montréal. I know Montréal surrendered quickly this *septembre* past, and I wonder what would have happened had we in Québec done the same. No matter. It is done.

But I digress. The funeral was one of great dignity, the Mass said by the Vicar General, Curé Montgolfier. Monsieur Bélanger had no family other than Mme Claire, but he did have many friends and admirers, being such an important and wealthy man. It is the reason the funeral Mass was held in the Basilica, I suppose, a building of amazing beauty. Later, Mme Claire said that many of the mourners reminded her of vultures, all hoping for a piece of something. They hoped in vain, for Monsieur Verges says that Madame's uncle has left his entire estate to the Church.

Le 3 décembre 1760

A note has arrived from Monsieur Verges. In it, he said that the Vicar General is permitting us to stay here as long as we wish. In spite of that, and in spite of the kindness of the servants here, Mme Claire has decided that we are to leave tomorrow. None of us is comfortable in this house. There is an air of waiting, which reminds me of last summer, when all of us at Québec awaited the arrival of the British warships.

But this is not a war, only a matter of Monsieur Bélanger's estate and possessions being turned over to the Church, which seems like so much business to me.

The note also said that Monsieur Verges will be coming here this evening, since Mme Claire has been left a small bequest from her uncle. Whether it is a jewel or a sum of money, none of us can guess.

Très tard

Monsieur Verges wasted no time on formalities this evening. His servants had finally located the bequest, and it was out in front of the house. We should bring it in quickly, he said, for it was prone to escaping, just as it had after Monsieur Bélanger's death. And Monsieur Verges suspected that the creature liked to bite — it might be a good idea to purchase a chain and a whip, if neither was at hand. Here were its papers. Then he left, wishing us all the luck in the world.

"What can it be?" Mme Claire wondered. Her uncle had not been fond of savage animals, as far as she knew. I recall that images of wolves and bears came into my mind as we left the *salon* and opened the front door. All I could see was Monsieur Verges, making a rapid retreat. It was then we heard a terrible scream come from the kitchen, and how I prayed to the Holy Mother of God that the cook was not being eaten alive.

She was not. But she was in a corner of the kitchen, having been forced there by a small and filthy boy of perhaps ten years, who was holding a chicken leg in one hand and a toasting fork in the other, one that he jabbed in her direction every few seconds while he tore at the chicken.

"His name is Luc Panis," said Mme Claire, peering at the boy's papers.

It told me everything. He was an *indien* slave, a *panis*, and he had been left to Mme by her uncle. My stomach tightened, for I loathe slavery, as does Mme Claire. Even indentured servitude is unacceptable in most cases, since the terms are often so harsh. What would we do with a *panis*?

"Sell him!" shouted the cook. "It has been peaceful here since that creature took to the streets. See that? The brat has already stolen food, and I know he would stab me like you do one of those English sausages, given the chance. Sell him, Madame, for if you do not, your life will be a misery! Why Monsieur Bélanger ever purchased such a little monster is beyond me."

That was when Chegual entered the kitchen, drawn by the shouting. He snatched the fork from the boy, who tried to run past him, but Chegual easily caught him and

Chegual came in but has now gone from my room. What a terrible tale of suffering he told me. Chegual made the boy a pallet in the kitchen and by now is also bedded down there. Later. I will finish this later.

The boy's name is Pitku. He does not speak — Chegual thinks it is from grief and sorrow — but signs with his hands using the trade language my brother used when he travelled in the West.

Le 8 décembre 1760
Le soir

Home at last to a joyful welcome from Wigwedi, La Bave and Cook. Andrew, we learned, was not in his quarters in our library, but attending the Governor on some military matter or another, and would be here later. I scarcely have the heart to write about what happened on the way here.

Tard

Mme's friend Lieutenant Stewart came to call, some hours after Andrew's return, bearing a cheese as a gift. It was a Gloucester cheese, we were told, one that had been made in England. Over the cheese and small glasses of port for the men, Madame Claire told them all that had occurred over the last week.

It saddened me to hear Pìtku's story yet again, how he had been the second-born of twin boys, his name being the Pawnee word for *two*. Of how the twins were of particular interest to the slavers who slaughtered all the adults in their village, and stole the children. Pìtku's brother had died on the trail, as did many others. I was certain that the horror of all this was the reason the boy never spoke.

"That he lived is a miracle," said the lieutenant solemnly, and I agreed. Then he asked if he might see the child.

"You cannot," my brother told him. "He ran away when we stopped for the night at Trois-Rivières."

How my heart ached for Chegual. Pìtku had been well-behaved as we journeyed along le Chemin du Roi, passing through Repentigny, St. Sulpice and Berthier. But then at St. Charles, the child had acted out, and when Pìtku kicked me — I am certain it was not intentional — my brother had scolded him severely.

I can still see Chegual's face that next morning when he realized Pìtku was gone. For two days he searched, offering the reward that Mme Claire was willing to pay, but to no avail. In the end, we left the inn and also left Pitku. All the way home, Mme Claire worried aloud about the poor boy we would have cared for until he was old enough to be freed. It would not have been slavery at all, but simply a means of keeping him safe and in one place.

Later, Andrew said that perhaps it was for the best, that Pitku may find his own way in life well enough. I pray that is so, but it still saddens me.

Plus tard

I have been thinking about the war. The British, for all their marching and drumming, have not been unkind. Our own civil laws remain, as do our churches. They also permitted people to keep their slaves, both negro and *panis*.

We lost so much during the war. Why could we not have lost slavery?

Le 9 décembre 1760

Sometimes I feel as though I have become a soldier. This household certainly keeps the same hours as the British garrison here in Québec does, which is why I am out of bed and writing in this diary. *Reveille* never fails to wake me. Sometimes, as I did today, I wake before the drumming and bagpipes begin, and lay in my bed waiting for the sound of them. I cannot help it. Even now, these many months after Québec was lost, I hope just a little that I will not hear them, that it will all have been a dream.

I keep thinking about the grand basilica still standing in Montréal, and then our own Notre-Dame-des-Victoires, destroyed by the British during last year's siege. It was a terrible thing, that siege. I must cease, though, and not give in to such foolishness. The British and *Les Écossais* are here for good.

But I return to my day, which was shopping for Cook this morning, as she refuses to do so herself since her poor English is an embarrassment to her. I cannot blame her for that, and so the task of purchasing our household goods falls to me. It is no hardship, and besides, work takes my mind away from Pìtku.

Mister — he prefers this — Mister Wharton is a fair man, and so it is his shop that I favour. So does Mme Claire. None of us can truly become used to the British and American goods, however, but they are all we can buy, since nothing at all comes from France anymore. Best not to complain, even in this journal, since at least we have food. I do not want to remember the hardships of last winter.

In the market, I heard a rumour that *Les Écossais* have taken a prisoner, one who attempted to steal bread from their bakery. They say that the penalty for theft is death. Food is precious, but a loaf of bread cannot possibly equal a life — even to *Les Écossais*.

La nuit

My earlier words, that the British and *Les Écossais* are here for good, are like a two-edged blade. It is hard in some ways, yet it also is good. That is because of Andrew, who has become so dear to us, but only in the privacy of this journal can I say how dear he is to me.

Le 10 décembre 1760

What a day this has been! It began as always, with *reveille*, but then as I lay abed, the sound of bagpipes seemed to grow closer. By the time I quickly dressed, the sound was right below my window and a glance below showed me Chegual and Andrew, with Lieutenant Stewart playing the bagpipes. A dozen other soldiers waited behind them in a close group.

"A loaf of your household's best bread," Andrew demanded, once Mme Claire, Cook and I stood before him. When I inquired why, he answered, "I will take it in trade."

That was when the soldiers parted to reveal what their bulk and their kilts had hidden. It was Pìtku. Pìtku, who had tracked us here to Québec, who had searched the town for us, and in desperate hunger had tried to take bread from *Les Écossais'* stores.

I remembered then how Andrew had told me about the hunger he had suffered after the Battle of

Culloden in Scotland. His mother had died from starvation. I knew in my heart that Andrew would never harm a starving child, and felt a great fondness for him overcome me. Then I saw his muddied knees and stockings.

"*La petite bête sauvage* should be renamed *La Mule*," he grumbled. "Best teach him manners, mademoiselle."

Later Chegual learned that it was the scolding at Trois-Rivières that made Pìtku decide to follow us after all. The boy used no words, but signed with his hands that Chegual's scolding had made him recall a memory nearly lost. Pìtku's father used to scold him and his brother that way. He had not cared for scoldings — who would? — but he had loved his father very much.

Although it was not said aloud, I understood then that Pìtku must be grateful to Chegual for helping to keep a precious memory alive. Poor child, to grasp at even that small shred of comfort.

Le 11 décembre 1760

It is necessary that Pìtku bathe, and then be deloused by Chegual, who

I cannot say I care much for the howling, or for

It seems that Pìtku has a strong dislike of soap and hot water. Still, the task was completed, and although Chegual and the kitchen were soaked, Pìtku was finally wearing clean clothing. With the layers of filth gone, I could see that he was a comely enough child. Cook cast somewhat doubtful looks at him, but she is a kind woman and I also saw looks of pity — Chegual would have told her Pìtku's story. And she had given Pìtku a knife — a rather dull one — with which he was peeling potatoes!

Le 12 décembre 1760

Perhaps *Not Tormenting Animals* should be added to the list of rules Chegual gave Pìtku yesterday, although I suppose the boy was only being playful. But when he tried to play with Wigwedi she was not pleased. She growled, which should have warned him, and then she nipped his finger. Later Wigwedi went into the kitchen and fouled Pìtku's pallet. It fell to me to wash out the urine, but I insisted that Pìtku help.

As for La Bave, she is a patient dog. I thought I knew her well, as she has lived with us since the siege, but this morning I learned something new when Pìtku tried to place Wigwedi on her back. La Bave does not consider herself to be a horse. Ah, well, he survived being sat upon by a heavy New Found Land beast, and possibly has learned a lesson.

Le 13 décembre 1760

Chegual signed to Pìtku that he must accompany me this morning. So he walked with me to Mister Wharton's shop, as we were short of salt, ink and a number of other things. It was how I learned that Pìtku is given to staring and pointing. I think it is because he is unable to express himself in any other way if Chegual is not with him. It was one thing for him to stare at common people, but when he stared at Mère Marie-Charlotte de Ramezay, my embarrassment was indescribable.

On the other hand, Mère Marie-Charlotte is a very tall nun, at least six *pieds*. When she is walking about the town on some business or other, she is easy to see in a crowd. They say that Governor Murray suggested she might like to become a *grenadier*, because of her height and her patriotism. I doubt that it is true, though.

Le 14 décembre 1760

Mass at the Ursuline chapel as usual. As I knelt, I recalled something that Mère Esther once told me, how one of the first Ursulines who came to Nouvelle France many years ago made an infant Jesus of wax for the *indiens* who visited their mission. I then began to think of Christmas, and in particular, of our *crèche*. It and its waxen figures of the Holy Family were destroyed last year when our house in the Basse-Ville burned.

When we walked home from Mass, I mentioned my musings to Andrew and Mme Claire. Andrew said that he recalled his grandparents' *crèche* from when he lived with them in France as a child. Mme Claire said that perhaps someday we would have another *crèche,* but it was out of the question for now.

Le 15 décembre 1760

Wonderful news! Mère Esther has been elected by the Ursuline sisters to be the superior of their convent. Mme says that Mère Esther is very deserving of the position. With our city now in the possession of the British, the nuns were very clever to have elected an American. After all, the American colonies are also British possessions.

Americans. I wonder if it is any easier for them to be British subjects than it is for us.

Le 16 décembre 1760

When I went to the kitchen to find a candle for the candlestick in my room, Cook remarked that Pîtku seems to be clever with his hands. He can peel a potato, leaving behind barely a sliver of white flesh. As for the candle, she added that we must get a cat, since the candles are disappearing, and that is a sure sign of mice. Odd.

Le 17 décembre 1760

The library has remained Andrew's chamber since last year when he was billeted with us. He and Chegual have begun spending evenings there with Pitku. None of us is to enter, since they feel that the company of men will do him good. Mme Claire says we must use the situation to our advantage, since we are secretly knitting mittens and stockings for all three of them as Christmas gifts.

Le 18 décembre 1760

La Bave and Wigwedi were admitted to the library tonight. That both are females seemed not to matter. I heard no growling, so I suppose it all went well.

As for Pitku, I believe his earlier behaviour was born of fear. He has nothing to fear in this house, though.

Le 19 décembre 1760

I have seen them! I have seen my brother and Pitku speaking together when they went out on an errand today. Their heads were together. It must have been speech.

Le 20 décembre 1760

Not a word from Pitku, only the same hand signs he and Chegual exchange. Perhaps my imagination overcame me.

Le 21 décembre 1760

When Mme Claire left the room to get more wool, I fear I spied. At least I spied with my ear, which I pressed against the library door. Laughter. I heard the sound of Chegual, Lieutenant Stewart and Andrew softly laughing. And I was certain I heard a fourth sound, one that was light and young, but it was at that moment that Mme returned and made a sound of her own. *Get away from that door, you nosy girl,* is what the sound meant.

Le 22 décembre 1760

Candles! As soon as one is replaced, it disappears. Has an army of mice and rats invaded our house?

Le 23 décembre 1760

Christmas Eve tomorrow. We are as ready for the festive season as we can be.

Le 24 décembre 1760

Tonight Andrew placed a small candle in every window of the house, explaining that it was *Les*

Écossais' tradition of *Oidche Choinnle,* which he has spelled for me. The candles will light the way for the Holy Family this Christmas Eve. They will also light our way home after midnight Mass. Chegual wondered aloud whether the candles might also guide the rats and mice to us, and we all laughed at that.

Chegual and Pìtku will not attend Mass. Instead, they will guard our meal of Cook's *tourtières* so that Wigwedi and La Bave do not begin the feast without us.

Le 25 décembre 1760
Le soir

This first day of the Christmas season was a happy one, and I know that the next eleven will grow happier as each day passes. Lieutenant Stewart came to help us celebrate. He and Mme are now Claire and Jonathan to each other in the privacy of this house, and it warms my heart to see the friendship growing between them. As does my friendship with Andrew.

Cook prepared a capon that she stuffed with bread and spices. There were potatoes, of course — always potatoes, which we once considered animal food. With butter and onions they go down very well. And an apple *tarte* that went perfectly with the cheese Lieutenant Stewart again brought. After the meal, we all sat in the *salon* to converse.

Not a word from Pìtku, although I saw his eyes

closely following each person — particularly Chegual — as they spoke.

Le 26 décembre 1760

La Bave has taken to sleeping with Pìtku, wrapping herself around him like a great, black bear pelt. It made me smile to see them tonight.

Le 27 décembre 1760

Several days ago, Mme received an invitation to attend a dinner party at the residence of Governor Murray in honour of the Christmas season. Lieutenant Stewart will escort her. I was included in the invitation, but I now have a streaming cold, which is quite unseemly. Andrew does not mind the streaming, and so he will keep me — rather, *us* — company this evening.

I loathe a streaming cold, but I do look forward to an evening with Andrew.

Le 28 décembre 1760

Andrew spoke of slavery last night. Many of his fellow Scots were sold into slavery after the Battle of Culloden. He despises the institution as much as I do, and yet he considers Pìtku to be a fortunate boy. "Until the day he is freed, he has a roof over his head, good women to watch him, an Abenaki warrior to act as his guide, and a fine dog for a companion," he told me. When I wondered whether Pìtku was happy here, he added, "I am certain of it."

If only Pìtku could say so.

Le 30 décembre 1760

It is odd how unfamiliar things can become ordinary, how new traditions become your own. Tomorrow night we will celebrate Hogmanay, something we had never heard about before *Les Écossais* arrived. We must *redding* the house, cleaning it from top to bottom, something of which Cook approves.

Le 31 décembre 1760
Au point du jour

Lieutenant Stewart was our first-foot visitor, as *Les Écossais* say. He stepped through our door just after midnight, bearing a bit of coal, a bottle of Scotch whisky, and some cups, shouting *"Lang may yer lum reek!"* It looks quite odd written here, but the thought is good, for if your fire smokes long, you will be warm and secure.

We served out *het pint* in the small cups that Andrew calls noggins, the mixture of eggs, hot ale and sugar tasting delicious. In all it was a most pleasant night, what with the sounds of revelry echoing through the town, and the quieter sounds of celebration in our own house.

1761

Mère Esther says that a tale should be told from beginning to end, and therefore I will do that here. So, after Mass, we women spent the day resting in anticipation of yet another evening of festivities. There were gifts to exchange, after all.

When the time finally came, when supper was in our bellies and the crumbs brushed from the table-cloth, Mme and I brought out the packages. Andrew, Chegual and Lieutenant Stewart exclaimed over our knitting. Even little Pìtku seemed pleased, although he only smiled his enjoyment.

Then, nothing.

The men turned to their pipes and sherry, the conversation resumed, and the evening proceeded. Mme seemed unaffected, but inside myself, I could not help but feel some disappointment that no thought had been given to gifts for us. It was followed by a wave of guilt.

I argued with myself about greed, and was winning the argument when Andrew said, "My journal, Geneviève. There is a page I wish to read aloud. Would you please get it for me?" No gift, and now I was being asked to fetch his journal. I grumbled inside myself and kept grumbling until I opened the door of the library.

There on the library table stood a simple *crèche*. The Holy Mother and St. Joseph leaned over a small manger in which lay the baby Jesus. A cow and a mule stood behind them. So did a rabbit and a large dog.

"It seemed right to add them," said Andrew, who came into the library with everyone else. And then the mystery was revealed. Pìtku had been charged with gathering all our candles, since Chegual believed the *crèche* should be made from part of the house. Cook had been assigned the task of planting the idea of mice in my mind. The evenings in the library? Those had been spent melting the wax, shaping it and then carving the figures — Pìtku's nimble fingers working busily — until each was exactly right. Even La Bave and Wigwedi, who had acted as models, had been part of the plan.

Nothing could have made me happier. But then something did, and my heart swelled with happiness!

"*Bonne Année*, Geneviève," said Pìtku slowly and carefully, and how I longed to take him in my arms as Chegual explained. They had not spent all their time playing with wax. Time was given to learning words and to talking, as well.

Gifts. They come in many forms. Friendship, thoughtfulness, and yes, even a few words. There will be more words, and many conversations, but for today, those three were more than enough.

CHARLOTTE BLACKBURN

NO SAFE HARBOUR

The Halifax Explosion Diary
of Charlotte Blackburn
Halifax, Nova Scotia
September 26, 1917 – March 24, 1918

By Julie Lawson

Charlotte and her brother Luke, a soldier serving overseas during World War I, frequently exchange letters. Charlotte fears for his safety, for the worst she can imagine is that Luke will not come home from the war. She's still a year away from knowing how her own life will be changed when a munitions ship in Halifax Harbour catches fire, causing the largest man-made explosion in history and flattening the city of Halifax.

When War Hits Home

Whitley Camp, England
December 7, 1916

Dear Folks,

Thanks a million for your last letter. It only took 11 days to get here!

This'll be a proper letter — no more army postcards, I promise — and it could be a long one, so I hope you're settled by the fire with a pot of tea handy.

We thought our training was over when we left Canada in October, but no sir, we've had two months of it here and more to come. Gosh, didn't we get it right the first time? Parades, inspections, drills, three forced-route marches a week (sometimes at night), shooting practice, bayonet practice, saluting till your arms drop off — but heck, that's army life. You don't ask questions, just follow orders.

Don't know when we're going to France but sure hope it's soon. We're itching to get into the action and do our bit! I know you're doing yours. Speaking of action, we're pretty close to the thick of it, what with airplanes and sometimes dirigibles patrolling the coast and big search-lights watching out for enemy aircraft and soldiers at a nearby camp practising on anti-aircraft guns. On a real clear day if we get up high enough, we can see across the Dover Strait to the coast of France.

Sundays we parade to church in the morning and have the afternoons free, unless we're on "fatigue." That means "chore." What Lame Brain thought that up?! Kitchen fatigue is pretty un-appetizing, mostly scraping out pots and pans or peeling spuds. Sure we grumble a bit, but heck, it's all in the game.

Saturday afternoons are free too, and I've had some good times in Godalming. I probably told you it's the closest town to Whitley Camp. The High Street's busy with Christmas shoppers and the shops are decorated with wreaths, just like at home. You can't beat the locals, the way they go all out for the soldiers. Free concerts every weekend

end with talent from London — the best darn shows I've ever seen — and free dances at the YMCA about once a week. Lots of pubs if you want some good grub and a couple of pints. And get this, they have barmaids! Of course there's always some Brass-Hats on duty making sure the troops don't have too much of a good time.

Yesterday I was "honoured" to be the stick guard man! You're wondering, what the heck — ? It means I was the best turned-out soldier on morning parade. Got a reward too! I was let off from formal parades and extra duties for 24 hours.

Just 20 minutes to go before my free time runs out, so better sign off. It's going to be some strange spending Christmas away from home, but we're all in the same boat over here, and we'll make things as merry as we can. I'm counting on you to do the same!

There's nothing beats mail from home, so keep those letters coming, take care of yourselves, and have a Merry Christmas. That's an order!

Your loving son and brother,
Luke

Blackburn Camp, Halifax
MY dear, ~~goofy~~, swell brother
I AM ~~brave~~, disloyal, ~~silly~~, confused
WE ARE busy getting ready for Christmas, ~~setting lobster traps~~, wishing you were here
I AM UP TO MY EYEBROWS IN ~~mud~~, worry, ~~haddock, maple syrup~~, kitchen fatigue
THE WEATHER IS rainy, snowy, undecided
THANK YOU for your letter
WOULD LIKE ~~a bayonet for Christmas~~, a letter from you that's just for me
YOUR loving ~~cousin, sweetheart~~, sister

Signature only *Charlotte Blackburn*

DATE December 16, 1916

Monday, December 18, 1916

Dear "Stick Guard" Luke,

We got your letter this morning and had a right good laugh about your new honour! Duncan even made a cardboard cutout of you as a Stick Guard to hang on our Christmas tree. Not on top, in place of the angel, but close enough. Mum says we need the angel watching over you.

I hope you like my army postcard. (I copied the form from the ones you sent, but made up the rest.) I wasn't going to send anything else, but you know me,

I have to write a letter too. We're *all* writing to you so you'll get lots of news.

Mum and Dad are in good spirits, but missing you something terrible. Mum's not touching the money you send from your pay. She says if the war goes on much longer there might be food rationing and prices will shoot up. Then the extra money will be handy. "It's for a rainy day," she says, and when I said, "It's raining hard enough today," she told me not to be sassy.

Duncan's been on Coal Fatigue since the beginning of December, bringing in extra hods of coal so Dad doesn't have to. He's thinking of Christmas, our Duncan, and hoping for a pair of skates from Santa, not a lump of coal. He even cut an ad out of the paper, and taped it to the icebox: SALE ON SKATES, 70¢ A PAIR.

I wouldn't mind a new pair of skates but I'd rather have another Anne book. *Anne of Avonlea* is the one that comes after *Anne of Green Gables,* and I've read that book three times.

Right now Duncan's colouring another Stick Man and guess where it's going? All you need, Luke — another soldier in your hut!

Every night Edith and I play Christmas carols, sometimes as duets. Mum likes to sing along while she's cleaning up after supper, and excuses me from Kitchen Fatigue. Not Ruth though, and she is some peeved! Yesterday Edith and I made maple fudge for

Christmas. You'll get some in the next parcel. (If there's any left, ha ha!)

Have you got our Christmas parcel yet? We mailed it on December 8.

Kirsty still runs circles around Duncan and me when we take her for a walk, and her tail never stops wagging. It's double time on her route marches!

Ruth has probably told you about her starring role in Richmond's Christmas pageant. She played the part of Daisy with so much wringing of hands — because her sweetheart was sent to the Front — it's a wonder she has any skin left. I have to admit Ruth was good at the role, especially since Daisy's sweet character was so unlike her own. Ruth would as soon wring her hands around someone's neck. Usually mine.

I sang in the choir at the pageant. All my favourite carols except "O Tannenbaum," because it's German. *Tannenbaum* is the only German word in the song, so couldn't we just change it to "O Christmas Tree?" I asked the director and was scolded for being disloyal to the troops. I felt so guilty I've stopped playing that carol at home.

Is it disloyal to have a Christmas tree, since it was a German tradition to begin with? I wonder.

You might have guessed from my postcard that I'm worried about something, and now I'll tell you what it is. Remember my friend Eva? I've always liked going to her place around Christmastime because her family's Christmas is so different from ours. For one thing, they have an Advent Calendar. Remember the Christmas before the War when Duncan and I made one? The calendar goes from December 1 to 24, and each day has a door with a picture behind it, like a Christmas scene or a symbol. Mum hung it in the kitchen and we took turns opening the little flap "doors" until it was Christmas Day. Remember?

Well last Sunday I had supper at Eva's. Her mum lit the second red candle on their Advent wreath (one for each Sunday before Christmas) and we sang carols, like "Silent Night." Mr. Heine accompanied us on the guitar. Then we helped her mum roll out gingerbread dough and made cookies in different shapes to hang on our Christmas trees. I didn't think I was being disloyal. But the next day at school Deirdre and Muriel came up to me and said they saw me leaving Eva's house and what was I doing, "socializing with the Enemy?" Didn't I know Mr. Heine was a traitor and a spy? Didn't I want to join their Girls Against Fritz Club? I *could* join the G.A.F., but only if I stopped seeing Eva. If I *didn't*, I'd be shunned.

The girls in the Club have meetings, write letters to soldiers and knit socks, like we do in the Junior Red Cross, and have parties. There's one at Deirdre's this Friday. They're not allowed to talk to Germans or shop at Mr. Heine's store because he sends money to relatives in Germany and they use it to buy weapons so their soldiers can kill ours.

People are always saying we have to do our bit and make sacrifices at home to help win the war. It doesn't seem like much, giving up butter for margarine and using every scrap of food. (Mum caught me throwing out a stale crust of bread and did I get a lecture.)

Well I'm trying to do my bit, Luke. I knit socks, roll up bandages, fill Christmas stockings and parcels for the soldiers — but I wanted to do more. So after what Deirdre said I decided to make a sacrifice and stop being friends with Eva.

But it was *awful* seeing Eva across the playground, standing all by herself, watching us. It didn't feel right, ignoring her like that, and the rest of the week was the same. But now it's the holidays and I won't need to see her every day.

The funny thing is, I never thought of Eva as being German. Actually she isn't, it's only her dad. He has an accent, but it doesn't mean anything to me and I never think of him as "Fritz." Still, it's true what Deirdre said, Eva has relatives in Germany. She used to show me the presents they sent.

You're probably wishing I'd sent only the postcard instead of rambling on with my troublesome thoughts, but of course you don't have to read all this. I just hope you're proud of me for giving up something important.

On Saturday the dockyard had a Christmas party for the workers' children. (Ruth fancies herself "too sophisticated" and stayed home.) Santa Claus made an appearance and handed out candies, nuts and oranges.

This week we're setting up our Christmas tree and decorating the house. Duncan's offered to do *your* job, hanging the tinsel so it's *straight*. Remember how Dad used to clown around and toss it onto the branches in clumps? There'll be none of that!

Have to go before the Post Office closes. Write soon!

Your sister,
Charlotte

Whitley Camp, England
December 23, 1916

Dear Folks,

A million thanks for the swell Christmas parcel that arrived last week. Did I obey your orders and save it for Christmas Day? Heck, no! The shaving set and stationery are just what I need, and as for the cake, candy, smokes, socks, soap and everything, I couldn't be happier.

All week we've been getting parcels and greetings from home. Talk about luxuries! We must have gotten at least 150 boxes of eatables and have been living mostly on cake and candy! And nuts, chocolate, cookies, canned meats, canned milk, tinned salmon, tins of jam and rounds of cheese. Non-eatables too, like good cigarettes, hankies — the list goes on.

The boys are swell at sharing their grub, except we're all holding back a few items for when we're at the Front. I reckon they'll be a godsend Over There. And I have to tell you, Mum — that big tin box of fruitcake you sent was a hit, moist and tasty, the way it'd be in our own kitchen. It "took the cake" for being the best of the lot. Stiff competition, too! (Must've been the extra ration of rum that someone added to the mix, eh, Dad!) You can bet I've put some of that aside!

Yesterday I was on Decorating Fatigue and we strung up some wreaths and bits of greenery in the Mess Hut, even decorated a Christmas tree that was donated by the YMCA in Godalming.

Must sign off. Merry Christmas and heaps of love to you all,
Luke

Wednesday, December 20, 1916

Dear Luke,

IMPORTANT!! Make sure you read my December 18 letter FIRST. (If you've got it.) Otherwise you won't understand this one.

Yesterday I was at the trolley stop with Deirdre and Muriel and who shows up but Eva and her brother, Werner. Eva says hello, but we *turned our backs* as if she wasn't there. I felt terrible, like I was a different person.

On the trolley it was worse. Some old men were talking loudly about the Huns in Canada and how the government should lock them *all* up. They were talking about the War Act (I think that's what they said), and saying it's one thing closing down the German schools and newspapers and making the Huns carry special papers, but it's another thing letting them live on our streets and eat our food, and on and on. And the whole time, Deirdre and Muriel were smirking and pointing fingers at Eva and I was so embarrassed I wanted to shrivel up and disappear.

Well after a few blocks Eva said something to Werner, and they stood up to get off, even though it wasn't their stop, and Eva unexpectedly called out, "Merry Christmas, Everybody!" People smiled and returned the greeting, even the old men (because of course they couldn't tell she was German), and I wanted to do the same.

The worst part is that Eva caught my eye before stepping down and, even though her voice had sounded cheerful (the way it does when you say Merry Christmas), her face looked so desperate sad I wanted to get off with her. But I didn't have the courage, not with Deirdre scowling beside me.

Ever since I joined the G.A.F. Club my stomach's been churning — you know, Luke, the way you feel when you've eaten something nasty. When I think about you and the war, well then it's not so bad because I feel that I'm doing my patriotic duty. It's just all the other times, when I'm thinking of Eva.

I'm sorry to go on like that.

You can look forward to another parcel soon. Mum's been doing more baking and I've made you a special batch of fudge.

Your loving sister,
Charlotte

London, England
December 30, 1916

Dear Folks,

Hold onto your hats, I'm in the "Big Smoke!" That's what they call London. You think we get fog in Halifax? It's nothing compared to here.

Spent Christmas Day at Whitley Camp and it wasn't bad, all things considered, but I sure missed you folks. The army gave us a Christmas feast of roast goose with mashed potatoes, followed by mince pie and plum pudding. We each got a parcel from the local Ladies Auxilliary (I pulled off a towel, soap and socks) and a Christmas stocking stuffed to the very toe from the Red Cross at home. And from a bunch of other sources, more towels, socks, cigarettes, chocolates — you name it, even pickles! It's good to know that folks are thinking of the soldiers.

I was lucky enough to get a three-day pass so have been in London to see the sights. The chaplain arranged for transportation, sightseeing and billets. A pal and I were put up by a friendly couple who treated us like kings.

London's full of soldiers and there's no end of entertainments — moving pictures, theatres, dances, concerts, pubs, restaurants — it's quite the high life I've been leading these last 3 days. And get this, I've even had a good hot bath!

Heard the darndest story about a truce in France the first Christmas of the war. It was Christmas Eve, and Tommy and Fritz no more than 30 or 50 yards away from each other, and when one side started singing carols, the other side joined in! They agreed not to fire, and before long, up and down the line, they were putting little Christmas trees with candles on the parapets and meeting in No Man's Land, laughing, joking, sharing gifts — even playing soccer, for gosh sakes! Can you imagine?

It would never happen now, not with all the casualties, but it makes me wonder what I would do if it did happen. Could I look Fritz in the eye and sing carols? Or toss him a soccer ball? Would I see a boy my own age? Or would I see a Kraut who'd mow me down without blinking an eye? When I get home, will I ever be able to see or hear a Kraut without thinking "Enemy"??

Gosh, listen to me go on! We're not supposed to THINK in the army. That's what comes of all this waiting.

Guess I should stop grumbling. We're training to be better soldiers, right? So when the time comes we'll do a better job of playing the game, no matter what our lot might be.

My wishes for 1917 are the same as yours, I reckon — *Victory for the Allies and a Blackburn Family Reunion!!!* Keep those letters coming, and have a Happy New Year!

Your loving son and brother,
Luke

P.S. January 2, 1917 Didn't post the above soon enough so here's more news. Yesterday we got a late "Christmas present" from the British Army — our Kitchener Boots! Know what that means? One, we can chuck out the falling-apart boots we got in Canada and two, *the time has come!* We'll probably get the boots well broken in before we tackle Fritz, but finally we'll see some action!!

January 1, 1917

Dear Luke,

Happy New Year! How was your Christmas?

We went to a special Christmas service in the morning and spent most of the day quietly at home, singing carols, reading *(Anne of Avonlea!)* and eating too much. We drank a toast to you at dinner. Mum tried to be merry but she took it some hard, your not being here. We reminded her that you're safe in England, not at the Front, and that cheered her some — until Ruth says, "Luke won't be missing us, Mum — he's probably still in London having the time of his life!"

Poor Duncan got his skates for Christmas, but there's no ice for skating. No snow, either.

Remember my last letter, about the G.A.F. Club? Well, Friday after supper I set out for Deirdre's party, got as far as her street and saw Muriel and some other girls going into Deirdre's house, as merry as could be, and I couldn't take another step. All I could think about was Eva.

So before I knew it I was at her door. I wouldn't have blamed her if she'd shut the door in my face, but she didn't. She didn't even let me finish my apology. She invited me in, and I joined her and her family for tea and gingerbread, and brought out the fudge I'd been taking to Deirdre's. And there we were, sitting at the kitchen table, laughing, chatting, making plans for the rest of the holidays as if nothing had happened. You can't imagine my relief! I walked home that night with my heart *almost* full of the Christmas spirit — *almost*, because the war is still on — but for sure I felt lighter in my heart.

Eva is a better and braver person than I am. And I can't stop being her friend, not on account of her dad. He's more Canadian than German now anyway, isn't he? I'm hoping the other girls will come round to the same way of thinking, but if they don't, they'll miss out on having a generous, forgiving friend.

Mum says she's proud of me for making the decision on my own. Duncan says I was stupid to join the Club in the first place, as if breaking a friendship could make a difference to the war. Mending our friendship made a *big* difference, Luke, so please don't think I'm a disloyal sort of person.

On Boxing Day Eva came over with a loaf of her mum's special Christmas bread. It's called *stöllen*, and it's full of nuts, raisins and other dried fruits. We sat down for cocoa and big slices of *stöllen* and everybody loved it, and afterwards Mum gave Eva some fruit-cake for her family.

We can't wait to hear about your Christmas. If you've written already, our letters might cross in the middle of the Atlantic. But if you haven't written, do it now and that's an order! (Duncan told me to put that.)

Our New Year's wish is for an Allied Victory before you leave England — no matter how much you're itching to get Over There. Wouldn't that be a wonderful beginning to 1917?!

Your loving sister,
Charlotte

Flora Rutherford

Days of Toil and Tears

The Child Labour Diary of Flora Rutherford
Almonte, Ontario
May 19, 1887 – February 14, 1888

By Sarah Ellis

Flora longed for a family of her own after living in an orphanage for almost ten years. She found one with her aunt and uncle, though she spent long hours at the woollen mill, where the work was sometimes dangerous. When that danger strikes close to home, it is time for yet one more move, and trying to get along with new relatives.

Reading Henry

December 10, 1888

Miss McPhee is getting married! She told us this morning just before the dinner hour. She is to marry Mr. Sutherland, who owns the feed and tack store in Kamloops. She showed us a photograph of him. He has a moustache but, thank goodness, no whiskers. I would not like to think of Miss McPhee marrying a man with whiskers.

After the news, Miss McPhee dismissed us and the boys just gobbled their dinners and roared outside to continue their snowball war. Even though there are now four boys in my family, I still find them mysterious. Have they no curiosity about interesting things? Of course, all the girls stayed in to ask Miss McPhee questions. Even cousin Martha, who cannot sit still and attend to her lessons, sat quiet as a mouse, listening.

The wedding will be on December 29. Miss McPhee is going to live in town in a house that Mr. Sutherland built, with plaster walls and a bay window.

(Bertha David asked if she would have lace curtains and Miss McPhee said she hoped so, by and by.)

When Mr. Sutherland decided he wished to marry Miss McPhee he wrote to her father who lives in Ontario to ask for her hand. (Martha asked why he just wanted her hand and Miss McPhee laughed and sorted that out. She is so good at explaining things and not just Geography). Mr. McPhee told Mrs. McPhee who told Miss McPhee's older sister who wrote to Miss McPhee's middle sister who is also a teacher and lives in Victoria who told Miss McPhee that Mr. Sutherland said that Miss McPhee was "his share of the world's treasure." Even though Miss McPhee's parents are sad that she will live so far away in British Columbia, they said yes.

Miss McPhee's middle sister is sewing her *trousseau*. Miss McPhee remembered that she was a teacher and wrote the word *trousseau* on the blackboard so that we would learn the spelling. Then she forgot she was a teacher and told us that everything was "scrumptious." She will have two nighties, two underskirts, four pairs of drawers and six slip-waists as well as dresses and a jacket. Imagine having that many clothes all new and all at the same time. And none of it made of old flour sacks, I'm sure.

Then Bertha asked if Miss McPhee would wear some of her scrumptious *trousseau* to school after she's married and Miss McPhee told us that she would not be coming back in the new year. Martha started to cry and I could have cried too. "I thought you understood that," said Miss McPhee. "Married women cannot be teachers." Then she gave Martha a hug.

We talked so long that Miss McPhee forgot to ring the bell and in the afternoon we had to skip sums. You would think that would make cousin Henry happy, because he has trouble with sums, but it didn't. On the walk home I tried to talk to him about the wedding but he was silent, as usual. Auntie Janet says he is shy, but he only seems to be shy with *me*. And how can he stay shy for so long? It has been *months* since we came west to join Uncle Wilf's family.

I am happy for Miss McPhee. But I'm sad for me. Will the new teacher be nice? And why can't married women be teachers? Back in Almonte nobody said that married women could not work in the mill. Even women who were expecting babies worked at the mill. I suppose being a teacher is more respectable. But getting married is also respectable. So wouldn't being a married teacher make you respectable times two? Life is not as tidy as sums.

December 11, 1888

I've just come in from the barn. If I were blind, I would always know the barn by the smell. Horses, dust, leather, hay and, this evening, whisky. Ollie is out there treating one of the horses who has colic. The treatment is laudanum, whisky and water. Ollie said he would have the *cayuse* right as rain by the morning. Ollie says "cayuse" instead of "horse."

Even though Ollie is just a cowhand he knows as much as a vet. Uncle Wilfred says that nobody can read the range like Ollie. Reading the range means that he can look at any field and figure out how many cattle can graze there and for how long. When he told me that, I thought of Mr. Houghton, the wool sorter back at the mill, and how he could "read" a fleece and know what sort of wool it would make.

Ollie likes to tell stories of the big cattle drives. "Weeks and weeks of bannock, beans, bacon and coffee." Tonight he told me how you can get cattle to cross a river. If it's spring, you rope the calves and put them in a boat and when the calves start bawling the other cows plunge into the river to follow them across. If it's fall, it is harder. You make a trail down a steep bank and get the cattle moving and then the cowboys have to scare the cows by hooting and hollering and banging rocks in cans to force the cattle into the cold water.

Uncle Wilfred says that Ollie can be very fierce when he drinks too much whisky, but I've never seen him fierce, only gentle with the animals, patient with explaining things and exciting when he tells stories. I suppose Miss Beulah Young and her Temperance ladies would try to make him sign the pledge and give up whisky for the rest of his life.

December 12, 1888

I told the news of the wedding over supper and everybody paid attention, but then Martha spilled her stew and baby Sadie started wailing, so Uncle James danced her around the room singing "There is a Tavern in the Town." Then Uncle Wilf started to talk about how there is going to be a baseball game on New Year's Day in Kamloops to celebrate an eclipse of the sun, and somehow the wedding was forgotten.

Before writing today's news in this diary I flipped back to read what I wrote in days gone by. So much has happened that it feels as though I'm reading a storybook, a story about a girl named Flora, who found a family and worked in a woollen mill and had a kitten named Mungo. A little girl.

When I looked back to this exact day a year ago I noticed that there was no entry for December 12 and I remembered why. This was the day that Uncle James had his terrible accident at the mill. Nobody seems to have noticed. Perhaps he and Auntie Janet *have* remembered, but are not saying anything.

When I see Uncle James rounding up cattle or

joshing with Ollie I can hardly remember the pale, angry man he was after his accident when the mill machinery mangled his hand.

If cousin Henry were friendlier I might talk to him about it. I know that a boy can be a good friend, because Murdo was. But Henry doesn't like me. I don't know why. I try to be kind. Sometimes I long for Alice and Mary Anne from the Home, or any girl my own age.

December 13, 1888

I thought I had imagined it but now I know. Henry is not just unfriendly. He hates me. We are doing long division in school. Miss McPhee tried every way to explain it to Henry but he just couldn't understand it. At supper Uncle Wilf asked about our day and I told everyone about long division and how I remembered how to do it from helping the boys at the Home. Then Auntie Janet said I was very good at household sums and figuring out if we could buy bacon, back in Almonte. Then Uncle asked Henry how he was getting on and Henry said that he hated long division and he hated school and then he stormed off to the barn. Auntie Nellie said she was hopeless at sums too and just to leave him be, but Uncle Wilf said Henry needed to do well at school to get on with life. Then he asked if I would help Henry. Secretly I thought that Henry might talk to me if we did long division together, so I said yes.

So Uncle Wilf fetched Henry from the barn and Auntie Nellie put a lamp at the end of the table and warned the little ones that they were not to bother us. I had a good idea. At least, I thought it was a good idea. I thought of Ollie and his story of getting cattle across the river. I tried to tell the story as well as he had. "So you come to a deep river and there is one boat. The river is icy cold and the cattle won't cross. So you rope the calves and put them in the boat. They are bawling and bawling for their mothers and finally, the other cattle plunge into the river. The cowboys are yelling and banging rocks in cans and the water is whipped into a foam. Here's the problem. The boat can only take seven calves at a time and you've got eighty-two. How many trips does it take and how many calves are left over for the last trip?" Then I wrote the numbers down as a long division sum.

First of all, Henry said that you can't fit seven calves in a boat. Then I said that he should *imagine* a boat that could take seven calves, or he could change it to five calves. Henry stared at the paper for a time and then he grabbed my wrist, hard, and whispered so nobody could hear, "Stop pretending to be a teacher. Stop being so clever." It was like he had declared war.

December 14, 1888

I am miserable. Henry won't even look at me. I don't know what to do.

December 15, 1888

I wasn't going to bother Auntie Janet, but this morning we had a minute to ourselves. The family went off to Kamloops for supplies. I like it when Auntie Janet is nursing Sadie because it means she stays in one place. I spoke right up. "Why does Henry hate me?"

I thought Auntie might say grown-up things like, "Oh, Henry doesn't hate you, what makes you think that?" but she didn't. She believes what I say. She just said, "Oh, you poor thing, I don't know." Then she told me about a woman in the weave room at the mill who took a dislike to her. "She treated me like poison ivy and I never knew why. Finally I decided just to pretend that we were friends. Sometimes if you pretend something is true, it becomes true." I asked if it worked and she said, "We never became bosom pals, but she did warm up a degree or two. We could at least work together."

Pretend something is true and it becomes true . . . I thought on that a while. I used to pretend fairies were true and they never were. Auntie Janet must have been thinking such thoughts too because then she said, "Mind you, for years I've been pretending to have raven locks and alabaster skin and last time I looked I still have brown hair and freckles, so it isn't foolproof."

But it is still worth a try.

December 16, 1888

This evening Uncle Wilf asked how Henry's long division lessons with me were coming and Henry just said "We're not doing that any more." He said it so fiercely that even Uncle Wilf did not know what to say.

December 17, 1888

Deep snow this morning. The uncles are having a long discussion about feeding the cattle. Uncle James thinks that they should be hauling hay for them, but Uncle Wilf says that cows can push their noses under the snow and eat the bunchgrass. The haystack is as big as a house but Uncle Wilf says it won't last that long — a haystack is like a bank account, and you can't spend it too freely. Then Uncle James said that all the children could be sent out to eat frozen bunchgrass and Martha said she wanted to try.

Miss McPhee has stopped being serious at school. Today we made Christmas presents. The girls sewed and the boys whittled.

On the walk home I tried to pretend that Henry

was my friend. Here are the things I talked about:

1. Favourite names for babies. My choices are Katharina for a girl and Alonzo for a boy. Henry has no favourites.

2. Whether it would be worse to be deaf or blind. Henry has no opinion.

3. Will we have a Christmas tree? Henry says yes. I suppose that counts as conversation with a friend. A very silent friend.

December 19, 1888

Today Miss McPhee invited all the girls and the mothers to come for tea on Saturday and view her wedding presents. She boards with Dr. Jenkins and Mrs. Jenkins, and Mrs. Jenkins is putting on the tea. Auntie Nellie says that Miss McPhee's people in Ontario are well off and that we will see some lovely things. Also, Mrs. Jenkins is known for her currant teacakes, so there is much to look forward to.

I asked my pretend-friend Henry if he was disappointed that the men and boys are not invited to the tea and if he thought that was unfair and if he liked currant teacakes and he said no, no and yes.

December 21, 1888

It was the last day of school before Christmas and the last day of school with Miss McPhee. We had no lessons at all but finished off our sewing and whittling while we sang Christmas carols and Miss McPhee read us a long story about magic and treasure called "The King of the Golden River." It was such a good story that even jumping-bean Martha sat still.

Then Miss McPhee told us that she knew we would work hard for the new teacher (they still don't know who it will be) and that she would miss us all. Then the girls cried and the boys didn't, but before we could get too sad Miss McPhee said that now she didn't have to worry about school inspectors ever again and that we should push all the benches to the wall to make room for games. We played tag and Red Rover and piggy in the middle.

I threw often to my "friend" Henry but he never threw back to me. Being in school and not behaving ourselves made us all feel quite wild and we got hot and loud and untidy and Miss McPhee joined in and her hair came down and she didn't even care. Finally we collapsed on the floor and had drinks of water and then Miss McPhee gave us bags of candy and sent us home early.

Martha ate her candy, piece after piece, all the way home. I made one humbug last the whole way and now I'm going to save the rest for Christmas day. Henry does not have a plan about eating or saving.

December 22, 1888

In "The King of the Golden River" there are two wicked brothers. They are cruel to their servants and they do not share with the poor and they hoard all their money. The story says that they had heaps of gold lying about on their floors. I feel that I have just seen a treasure house like that. Of course, Miss McPhee isn't wicked and her wedding presents were not lying about on the floor, but nicely arranged on the Jenkinses' dining room table. But I still feel that I have been to some magic world. There were sheets and handkerchiefs and pillow slips, a big painting of the ocean in a golden frame, a dark green leather case for keeping pens and paper, a red satin quilt, a Chinese tea set, lamps, vases, a clock for the mantel and so many things in silver, like knives, forks and spoons and cake baskets, pretty cups and saucers, a butter dish and a dressing-table set with a mirror, brush and comb. Mr. Sutherland gave her a golden watch that you wear pinned to your dress.

Everything was admired and discussed and everything had a story. We found out all about Miss McPhee's family in Ontario. Her mother is sad that she has decided to settle out West. "She fears that it is not civilized," said Miss McPhee. "But I'm a British Columbian now!" I thought of Miss McPhee lobbing the beanbag overhand across the classroom yesterday, her hair falling around her ears, and I wondered what being civilized meant. It would be lovely to have a house full of shining silver and a little gold watch to glance down on, but I don't think married ladies, even in British Columbia, get to play Red Rover very often.

The currant teacakes were heaven.

December 23, 1888

Great howling snowstorm last night. I woke up in the middle of the night because something was banging against the house and, once awake, I started to think how much I wanted to give Miss McPhee a wedding present. I could crochet her a doily or perhaps two if I'm not given too many tasks before Christmas, but then I thought of all those linens and silver and things from shops and I felt discouraged. I'm not that good at crocheting and a doily or even two is going to seem like almost nothing. I'm better at knitting, but it does not seem as though you give somebody a tam or muffler for their wedding, even if I did have the time to make one. And I don't have money to buy anything splendid.

I could have asked Auntie Janet and Auntie Nellie for an idea, but they are in a huge furor of baking and cleaning for Christmas. So I laid my problem at the feet of my friend-to-be, Henry. He was whittling and did not appear to be attending.

"Oh, little town of Bethlehem, how still we see thee lie." We sang this hymn yesterday. But that would be the opposite of Christmas here on the Duncan ranch. One word for Christmas: noisy. Two of the presents were for all the children to share. One was a puppy. Uncle James brought him in from the barn first thing. He is a small, roly-poly, brown and white dog with enormous ears and feet. Sometimes he trips over his ears and sometimes he trips over his feet and he loves to bark. The other present was a little cart that Uncle Wilfred made. The little ones took turns pretending to be a horse and pulling the others around the room until the cart turned over and everyone fell out. In the moments between these two ruckuses there was the sound of Martha playing her new tin whistle (nobody would admit to giving it to her), Sadie crying (she is too little for Christmas to be a treat) and Auntie Nellie singing.

There was also a new noise from me. I had the most scrumptious present. Auntie Nellie gave me her mandolin. "It's not my time for plunking and it is a shame for an instrument to go unplayed." I've never owned something that was so real and grown-up and beautiful. It is three kinds of wood with ivory pegs and mother-of-pearl decorations. It has its own case, which it fits into perfectly. Auntie Nellie said she will teach me to play. "When the little ones grow up we can have our own orchestra."

On Christmas Day I learned the D chord and how to play "Row, row, row your boat." Today I learned the G chord. Tomorrow I will learn the A chord and Auntie Nellie says with three chords I can play hundreds of songs.

I want to do nothing all day, every day, except play the mandolin. (And eat gingerbread, which must be the nicest food ever invented, second to currant teacakes.)

Today there was another great surprise. Henry spoke to me, not in answer to a question but all on his own. He says that he has an idea about a wedding present for Miss McPhee. But he won't tell me what it is. I reminded him that we only had one day and asked if we needed to get busy making something and he said no. Then I asked if we needed to get to the general store to buy something and he said no again. What kind of present is not bought or made? This is like a riddle.

December 27, 1888

The tips of my fingers are sore with mandolin playing, but Auntie Nellie says they will toughen up. I can almost play "Grandfather's Clock."

Henry is still being mysterious about the present for Miss McPhee, but he is definitely up to something. I saw him whispering to both the uncles and to Ollie and then they all grinned.

I haven't figured out the riddle of the present but I think I have figured out the riddle of Henry. He doesn't like to *accept* help. He likes to *give* it.

December 29, 1888

Weddings are lovely! I remembered the comical pretend wedding at the mill last year where all the men dressed as women and I got to be the minister. This wedding was not comical except for the very end, and that is when the secret of our present was revealed.

When the bride and the groom came out of the church the wagon was waiting for them. It was decorated with ribbons and the horses were perfectly groomed and all the harness cleaned and oiled and shining. Mr. Sutherland lifted Mrs. Sutherland *(Mrs. Sutherland!)* into the wagon and then Henry and Joe David popped up and started unharnessing the horses.

At first I thought Henry and Joe David were just being naughty, but then the uncles started to laugh and to help them. Then Uncle James led the horses away and the boys grabbed the traces and began to pull. At first the wagon did not move and then Henry called out, "Flora, come and lend a hand!" and I looked at Auntie Janet and she just nodded, so I put my shoulder to the side of the wagon and off we went.

There was great cheering and a rain of rice and old shoes. Along the way it started to snow, just lightly. Henry kept looking over his shoulder and grinning at me. We pulled the wagon all the way to the new house. Mr. Sutherland laughed and Mrs. Sutherland laughed and cried and said it was the best wedding present of all.

This evening we could not stop talking about the wedding. We were supposed to be sewing but not many stitches were stitching. Auntie Nellie said that pulling the newlyweds home is a mark of community esteem.

"That was a splendid idea, Henry," she said, "How did you think of it?"

"It was Father's toy cart," said Henry. "People pulling people. But Flora thought of the present idea in the first place."

"Ah, Flora," said Uncle James. "Her shoulder to the wheel made all the difference."

"Yes," said Henry, "Flora makes a fine *cayuse.*"

I could have knocked him on the head with my thimble, but I'm going to save that pleasure for a surprise.

The little ones are asleep now and it is so quiet that I can hear the hiss and pop of the fire and the puppy snoring in his basket. Day is done, as Mr. Longfellow would say, and this *cayuse* is going to bed.

Jenna Sinclair

Where the River Takes Me

The Hudson's Bay Company Diary
of Jenna Sinclair
Fort Victoria, Vancouver's Island
August 31, 1849 – May 2, 1851

BY JULIE LAWSON

After growing up at bustling Fort Edmonton
on the Prairies, Jenna found it hard to follow
the stricter rules at the more "civilized" Fort Victoria.
Even with new friends and different family ties,
she still treasures her exciting make-believe world
of Villains and Heroes. Adventure is never far
from Jenna's mind . . . and sometimes it erupts
right into her life.

The Daft Days of Christmas

Thursday, December 23, 1852

The Daft Days are coming! Our fattest goose is hanging in the storeroom alongside a haunch of venison, and our invitations have gone out for Christmas dinner. And for the first time I will be having it in a real *home,* and not in a Hudson's Bay Company fort.

In the forts we had a special dinner and a holiday on Christmas Day and saved the festivities for Hogmanay. But Uncle Rory decided that since he's now an independent settler and retired from the HBCo, we can celebrate both Christmas *and* Hogmanay.

I'm looking forward to midnight on Hogmanay, wondering who our first visitor in the New Year might be. Aunt Grace says the first-footer who crosses our threshold — we actually have a threshold now! — must be a dark-haired man, for any other is a bad omen. It's also a bad omen if the first-footer comes empty-handed. He has to bring an offering. In Scotland it's usually shortbread, whisky and a piece of coal, and the first-footer says, *"Lang may yer lum reek,"* which means, "Long may your chimney smoke." Aunt says it's a way of wishing the household a prosperous year, with plenty of food and drink and a good warm fire. As long as I can remember, the days between Christmas and Hogmanay have been called the Daft Days. I thought it meant "crazy," because of the tomfoolery that went on in the forts, but Uncle says it means "foolishly, frivolously merry."

Even wee Annie is caught up in our "daftness," tho' it doesn't take much to make her merry. Her favourite game these days is being bounced on my knee while I chant nursery rhymes, and *correcting* me when I make mistakes. (Which I do on purpose, to make her laugh.) When I sing, "The Daft Days are coming and Annie's getting fat!" she squeals, "No!" and babbles something I take to mean *"Christmas* is coming, the *goose* is getting fat!" She's very clever for 19 months.

Last week she helped set up the little figures for our *crèche* scene. She placed Baby Jesus in the manger with great tenderness, and was upset when later — to cheer her up after a fall — I removed Baby Jesus and put in a cow. "No," she shouted, and smacked my hand!

She loves hearing the Christmas story, and can point out Mary and Joseph, the shepherds, the angels, the three Wise Men and even the Star of Bethlehem (which I cut out of tin and fastened to the roof of the stable). She can say their names, too.

Our preparations for the Daft Days began over a year ago, when Aunt decided she wanted to make a plum pudding for *next* year's Christmas. Good thing she decided before the Home Ship left Victoria, as she had to order the currants and raisins from London. They arrived with the spring shipment and were hidden away until November 21, the Sunday before Advent. It's called "Stir-up Sunday" because the Collect for the day begins, "Stir-up, we beseech thee, O Lord, the wills of thy faithful people." But it's not only the people who get stirred up, it's the plum pudding!

The best part was "stirring up" and making a wish. We all had a turn, even Uncle and Annie, stirring from east to west, in the direction the three Wise Men were travelling. Annie wished for pudding!

After the "stir-up" came the "drop-in" — a silver coin (good luck for whoever finds it) and a button (bad luck if the finder's a man, for he is doomed to remain unmarried) — then came the "wrap-up" and boiling, and now it's safely stored away until Christmas.

My surprise for the family is safely "stored away" in the woods, but only until tomorrow. I pray it does not snow overnight or I will be hard pressed to find the exact spot!

Today I'm gathering evergreen boughs to place over the window tops and the mantelpiece. Uncle ordered a box of cranberries from Fort Langley and I've been stringing them to wind around the boughs.

There's the kettle whistling — time for breakfast.

Friday, December 24

A morning of chopping, sawing, hauling, hammering — all done in a rush to prepare my surprise while everyone was out.

First, off to the woods to cut down the tree (a little fir I picked out weeks ago).

Haul it to the barn and stash it behind some hay bales.

But how would the tree stand up? It couldn't lean in a corner — it needed a stand.

Off to the woodshed, find a wide board, saw it in half.

Off to Uncle's workshop for hammer and nails, then nail boards together to form a cross. Miss nail, hit thumb (several times). Hammer a circle of nails in the centre to support the tree.

But would it fit? Should have measured the tree trunk first.

Take stand to tree and, lo and behold, it's perfect.

As it happened I needn't have rushed. Aunt and Uncle were delayed and I had an hour to spare.

Christmas Day at Shady Creek Farm

9:00 p.m. and I am *finally* able to record the events of the day.

So, to begin. I crept out around 2:00 a.m. to fetch the tree, my plan being to have it set up in the parlour and decorated before anyone was awake. I'd finished hanging my little tin stars and was trying to figure out how to attach the candles, when in came Uncle Rory with a wooden horse he'd made for Annie. We took a moment to admire each other's handiwork and whispered how good we were at keeping secrets.

I returned to bed, my problem still unsolved. But when I got up again, some three hours later, what did I discover? My tree was aglow with candlelight! Aunt Grace and Annie were with me, and the three of us stared in awe.

Dear Uncle Rory! He'd gone to his workshop after I'd retired, made tin holders for my candles and fastened them onto the branches, thus turning my surprise for the family into a surprise for me.

When Aunt asked where I'd gotten the idea of a Christmas tree, I said, "From Queen Victoria."

She didn't believe me until I told her about a picture I'd seen in a London newspaper, showing the royal family around a Christmas tree. "Prince Albert took the custom to England from Germany," I said knowingly, and explained how Lucy had spotted the picture at school last year, when we were leafing through the newspapers that had come on the Home Ship.

By 2:00 our Christmas guests had arrived, all in their Sunday best. To make room for everyone, Uncle had extended our table by placing wide boards on sawhorses and spreading cloths over top. No one minded that one half was several inches higher than the other. Benches and packing crates served as extra chairs. As for the feast! A huge roast of venison and two wild geese (one brought by the Sullivans), mounds of potatoes, onions, carrots and turnips, Mrs. Sullivan's bread (fresh-baked this morning), butter from Esquimalt Farm and large decanters of Mr. MacLeod's blackberry wine. Everyone was in high spirits, passing pepper if someone asked for salt, or cranberry chutney if someone wanted butter.

Then the plum pudding! Aunt poured rum over top, set it aflame and carried it in to cheers and applause. Mrs. Sullivan found the silver coin and old Mr. MacLeod, a bachelor, found the button. "But Jenna," he teased, "I had my hopes on you!"

When the last spoonful was eaten, we raised our glasses and drank a toast "to absent friends." My eyes welled up, thinking of Father and Nokum smiling down from Heaven. I thought of Suzanne, too, far away in Fort Edmonton — oh, how I miss them! After dinner, the tables, etc. were moved out of the way and

Mr. MacLeod took out his fiddle. We played Charades and Blind Man's Buff, and danced a good number of lively reels. By this time Aunt had made a hot wine punch so the hilarity continued for another few hours.

Now I'd best try to sleep. Uncle wants to attend Rev. Staines's Service tomorrow, so we're off to Fort Victoria first thing in the morning. I'm not keen on the Service, but most eager to see Lucy, Sarah and other friends from school, even Radish.

Sunday, December 26

I'm writing this entry on paper that Radish tore out of his journal. (I should say, *Edward*, for he no longer wants to be called by his nickname.) Imagine, *Radish* keeping a journal! That's as surprising as the snow.

Yes, SNOW!

It started this morning during Rev. Staines's Service, and by mid-afternoon there was a good two feet. So here I am, stranded at Fort Victoria, and having a grand time with my former classmates.

Uncle and I left early this morning, as soon as he'd hitched Dickens to the wagon. It took a while to reach the Fort — we kept meeting people on the road and stopping to chat! — but we arrived on time for the Service. It wasn't too tedious though, since I could look out the window and watch the falling snow.

By noon it was falling so thick and heavy we could not even see the bastions! Uncle was anxious to get home to Aunt Grace, for she was feeling tired this morning after yesterday's exertions — as was Annie — but the snow was so deep, the wagon wheels kept getting stuck. Eventually he decided to ride Dickens and leave me at the Fort, promising to return for me when the road was passable. Then we'd load up with provisions and go home in the wagon. I told him not to rush back on my account, for I was content to stay with my friends.

Once he'd ridden off, I spent the rest of the day larking about in the snow and gossiping in the dormitory. Lucy and Sarah are as excited as I am about the Langfords' *soirée* on New Year's Eve, not only because the Langfords host such wonderful parties, but because they always invite the officers and midshipmen from whatever ship happens to be in port. (Right now it's HMS *Thetis,* which I saw sailing into Esquimalt Harbour). We made speculations as to whose future husband might be at the *soirée,* and Lucy says, "It won't be Jenna's — she's as particular as her Aunt Grace in choosing a husband." I reminded her I was only fifteen, tho' that is hardly too young for marriage, but the truth is, she's right!

At one point the subject turned to Radish. (I am too used to that name, so will not change to Edward.)

Lucy told me he writes stories in his journal, and said I should ask to read them. "He's sure to let *you*," she says. "Adoring you the way he does."

I scoffed at that — Radish is only *nine* — but she and Sarah assured me it was true, and we were soon laughing at his expense. The way he'd tag along with me when the boys were picking on him, how his stories always had a heroine named *Jenna*, how he'd once given Mrs. Staines the most preposterous excuse for his tardiness, using words that were straight from a story *I* had written.

Did he think of me as his big sister or as his mother, we wondered. Did he fancy me as his future wife? And more of the same nonsense.

We changed to another topic after a while, realizing that we were being unkind. Radish was lonely, he missed his family and wanted a friend — feelings that all of us can well understand.

Now more things are coming to mind, especially from my first year at Staines's School. There was the time I made him the hero in my brush-with-death story, and used his full name, Edward Radisson Lewis. How he beamed when I read it to him! Was that *adoration?* I just thought he liked the *story.* As for keeping a journal, in the two years I've known him he has *hated* Writing, Spelling, Grammar — everything. But Lucy was right, he was thrilled to show me his journal.

He's writing stories instead of recording daily events, though — otherwise, he says, every page would be *I hate school.* Maybe so, I told him, but school must be doing him some good, for his progress was remarkable.

He read me a story he'd written about a chief trader who beat his children so badly that one night the youngest decided to run away. He escaped by canoe but a storm came up and swamped the canoe, etc. etc. It was a thrilling adventure story and I told him so.

"I learned from you," he said, reminding me of the stories I'd written (and told). "It's no fun here now that you're gone."

"From the sounds of your story, you've taken my place," I said.

His face lit up with delight.

Must end and get ready for bed. No spares in the dormitory so I'm sharing with Lucy. We can whisper all night!

Monday, December 27
Before Breakfast

What a night! The dormitory beds are scarcely big enough for *one* person, let alone two, and Lucy — she kicked, elbowed, tossed and turned, rolled over and back, hogged the blanket, snored — I could have throttled her!

I don't expect Uncle to come today. Tho' the snow

has stopped falling, it's still too deep for the wagon, and the situation could be even worse out our way.

After Breakfast

The Fort is in a frenzy! Cecilia Douglas is marrying Dr. Helmcken this morning but she's at home across the Bay and he is *here!* The wedding *has* to take place before noon (because that's the law) and the carriage that's meant to fetch her keeps getting stuck in the snow!

Later

It is five minutes past noon and the wedding has taken place on time — thanks to the clever *canadien* who abandoned the useless carriage and fashioned a sleigh from a dry-goods box. He cut off the top and one side, put in a seat and covered it with red cloth. Then he made a shaft and runners from a couple of willows, set the box upon the runners, harnessed the horse and off they went to fetch the bride.

Goodness, it was a close call! Eleven ... half-eleven ... At a quarter to twelve, Lucy and I were peeking into the hall and saw a man trying to put back the hands of the clock! (But Mrs. Staines caught him.)

With ten minutes to spare we heard the jingle of sleigh bells and, lo and behold, the bride and her bridesmaids arrived. They rushed into the hall and the ceremony took place — I swear Rev. Staines has never spoken so quickly — and Dr. Helmcken put the ring on Cecilia's finger as the clock was striking twelve.

What a glorious clamour! Everyone in the yard shouted hurrahs as the party left to celebrate at Governor Douglas's house, the cannon roared from the bastions, the bell rang, the men fired muskets into the air and every dog for miles around howled as insanely as usual.

Early Afternoon

The excitement of the past 24 hours has got me as stirred-up as a plum pudding. So now that I've had Dinner, I'm going to walk home. I may still meet Uncle on the road — perhaps *he's* devised a sleigh! Anyway, I do not relish another sleepless night. So, a few goodbyes and I'm away. I have a good three hours before it gets dark.

Tuesday, December 28
Mid-afternoon

I'm back to my own journal and my "Stranded at the Fort" entries have been pasted in. Now, to continue.

I arrived home only this morning, as the journey turned out to be more eventful than I'd expected. Aunt and Uncle were none too pleased that I hadn't waited for him at the Fort, and even less pleased that I'd taken the path. "What were you thinking?" Uncle said. "What if I *had* gone to fetch you and hadn't seen you on the road, then found out that you'd left the Fort?"

After apologizing, and admitting that I'd acted impulsively, I gave an account of my journey. I explained that by the time I'd crossed the Gorge, I was tired of sinking into the snow (there were few tracks to step into) and was thinking the path would be quicker. Since the trees alongside the path were so thick, I reckoned their branches would have collected most of the snow before it could reach the ground. And I *had* considered Uncle and how worried he might have been, but since the road was impassable as far as wagons were concerned (not a single sign of a wheel), I thought it unlikely that he would have gone to Victoria, especially not so late in the day, and I figured he would not have wanted to make the trip again, only to return without the wagon and provisions.

A short time after leaving the road, I sensed that I was being followed. The back of my neck felt prickly, my heartbeat quickened. I heard sighs and moans, muffled thumps, rustlings in the branches tho' there was no wind. I kept turning around, even called out a few times — but saw nothing.

I told myself it was only a deer or a bird. But what if I was being stalked by a panther? Or by a murderer?

For I'd remembered that the men who'd murdered the HBCo shepherd in November were still at large.

As the shadows grew longer I became even more fearful. I had lost my way, I was still being followed, and my attempts to hasten only caused me to stumble and fall, expecting at any second to be pounced upon. Time and again that feeling of terror drove me on.

By the time darkness fell I was probably delirious, for when I saw lights in the distance, I imagined they were a host of angels coming to guide me home. I was singing their praises when a figure —

Oh, here's Annie wanting attention. Will continue later.

Later

The "angel" was Mr. Langford! What with all my stumbling, etc., I'd taken a wrong turn and ended up very nearly at his doorstep. He'd stepped outside on hearing the sounds of someone in distress (I thought I'd been singing!), found me lying in the snow and carried me inside. Mrs. Langford and the girls gave me some dry clothes to change into and warmed me up with tea and beef broth.

The food revived me enough to tell them that I was on my way home, but they wouldn't hear of my leaving.

It was going on eleven, I was more than half asleep and Mrs. Langford insisted I stay the night. "No point disturbing your aunt and uncle at this late hour," she said. "Especially since they're not expecting you."

After breakfast this morning, Mr. Langford lent me a horse to ride home and Mary and Emma accompanied me. I'd had a good sleep and was in a jolly mood, chatting with them about this and that, but mostly about their New Year's Eve *soirée*. We were making so merry, I did not even think of my mysterious stalker or whether he was still following me. In fact, being somewhat tired and fretful at the time, I'm beginning to think I imagined the whole thing.

Wednesday, December 29

Quelle surprise! I took Annie to the barn to give Dickens a carrot and what do we discover? Radish! Wrapped up in a horse blanket, sound asleep in the hay — but with his nose twitching like a rabbit's because of the straw. I almost laughed out loud.

Well, Annie takes in the scene and, no doubt thinking it's a larger version of our *crèche*, squeals, "Baby Jesus!"

"Shhh, don't wake him," I whispered, for I did not want Aunt to know about Radish until I figured out what to do. "It's a secret."

"Shhh." She grinned, delighted to share a secret, and we tiptoed away.

Back inside, she tugged Aunt's hand and started

chattering about Baby Jesus sleeping in our hay. Some secret! But Aunt, thinking Annie wanted to hear the Christmas story, took her to the *crèche* and obliged — leaving me free to gather up some food, blankets, etc., before returning to the barn.

"Radish!" I said, shaking him awake. "What are you *doing* here?"

It took him a moment to come to his senses. Then, recognizing me, he blubbered, "I followed you!"

"That was *you?*"

I suppose I spoke crossly, but I refused to be swayed by his tears. "Do you know how much you scared me? I thought you were a murderer!" And I demanded an explanation.

Well it turns out that the story he read from his journal was true — his father beat him, he ran away, etc. And any day now, his father is arriving in Fort Victoria to take him home to Fort Simpson, where he will once again be subjected to "the stinging fury" of his father's belt. So when he saw me leaving the Fort he followed me, spent last night in the Langfords' stable and ended up here.

I pointed out that his father couldn't be *that* cruel, since he'd sent him to school to get an education, but Radish said school was his mother's doing. She'd sent him when his father was away, to protect him.

By then my anger had given way to sympathy. I told

him he was brave to have run away, but he could not hide forever or stay in the barn. Aunt and Uncle had to be told *and* the people at the Fort — they'd be worried, and would be out looking for him. He sniffled some more, but admitted I was right.

I told Aunt and Uncle, and Uncle has gone to the barn to bring Radish in before he freezes. And now I've come to realize that I played a part in his running away. The "stinging fury" of his father's belt was a description I'd used in a story, about a boy who runs away from a horrible school to escape "the wrathful stinging fury of the Master's belt." I wrote it for Radish — he was wretchedly unhappy at the time — and he liked the story so much he practised the words until he could read it perfectly.

Later

Radish looked a sight when he came inside, his eyes ringed with dark shadows and red from crying, bits of straw sticking out of his hair and ears and clothing. He was shaking from cold and exhaustion. Aunt got him into a bath and gave him a bowl of hot broth. I'd no sooner set up a bed for him, than he was in it and asleep.

Uncle's on his way to Fort Victoria with news of the runaway, and to ask if Radish might stay with us until Hogmanay.

Moments ago we were awakened by a knock at the door. "Who goes there?" says Uncle, and I hear a man reply, "Charles Lewis."

Radish's father! I grabbed my robe and rushed downstairs, calling out to Uncle to send him away, saying he was a wicked man and would bring Radish to harm. But too late — he was already indoors and shaking Uncle's hand! And when he turned to me, offering a pleasant smile and apologizing for the lateness of the hour, I saw not the face of a brute, but of a kind and gentle man.

Meanwhile, Radish had heard the voice. "Papa!" he cries and hurls himself into his father's arms.

"Stinging fury" of the belt? I was dumbfounded! And so annoyed at having been taken in, I came up to my room without saying good night.

December 31

Radish and Mr. Lewis stayed overnight and have just left for Fort Victoria. They will return to Fort Simpson on the coastal ship in a few days time.

And Radish ("wee Eddy" to his father) is as happy as a clam at high tide. I confronted him after breakfast, telling him how embarrassed I'd been, trying to keep Uncle from opening the door. "I did it to protect you!" I said. "To save you from a beating!"

"But none of that was *true*," he says blithely. (Not a hint of embarrassment on *his* part.) "I made him into a Villain so he'd be more interesting. Like you do, when you're making up stories."

"But if he was coming to take you *home*, why did you run away from school?"

"Because he *hadn't* come and I was afraid he'd forgotten. You know how much I hate school, so I did like you said. Remember, when you wrote the story about a boy called Edward running away? I thought it was a secret message! I thought you were telling me to run away, but you were hiding it in a story so no one would know. I was proud of myself when I figured it out, Jenna. I only did like you said!"

Well, dumbfounded again. From now on, I'd better be more careful with my storytelling.

11:30 p.m.

What a wonderful *soirée!* Everything was perfect, except that I left behind the lace shawl Aunt lent me to wear. How could I be so careless? The excitement, the gaiety, the rush to be home by midnight, I suppose — well, there is no excuse. I must fetch it first thing tomorrow, before Aunt knows it is missing — provided she does not ask for it tonight.

Tho' I hated to leave the Langfords', I am glad to be here, for Hogmanay celebrations are in full fling downstairs and I am eager to join in, as soon as I finish this entry.

I knew everyone at the *soirée* except for the midshipmen and officers from the *Thetis*. What a lively, gallant lot! Lucy and I flirted shamelessly (as did the other young women, especially those nearing twenty) but we did not take to any one in particular.

The music was splendid, with Mrs. Langford playing her piano, two fiddle players and a middie joining in on his harmonica. We danced numerous reels and waltzes and later on played Blind Man's Buff. The game was more difficult than usual, for with the constant arrival of new guests, it was near impossible to tell who was who! The person I nabbed during my turn as It was a middie — I could tell by the buttons on his jacket — but I could not guess his name. I finally admitted defeat and pulled off the blindfold. "James Farraday," he says, and a more dashing young man I had not seen all evening. But by then it was 10:30 and time for me to leave.

"May I have at least one dance?" he pleaded, but I declined. I would not miss Hogmanay for the sake of a dance!

January 1, 1853
5:30 a.m.

Our first-footer arrived as we were singing "Auld Lang Syne," and who should it be but James Farraday! He has dark hair (a good omen) and did not come empty-handed (another good omen). But instead of bringing shortbread, whisky or coal, he brought Aunt's shawl! (Lucy noticed that I'd left it behind, and James kindly offered to return it.)

Well, in he comes and introductions are made. Uncle offered him a dram, and we all joined hands for another round of "Auld Lang Syne." Then Mr. Mac-Leod picked up his fiddle for more dancing. The candles on our Christmas tree flickered and shone, the tin stars gleamed and the merrymaking continued until the "last-footer" went home. I was hoping it would be James Farraday, but alas, it was not. He left as our clock was striking one — a good three hours before our festivities came to an end — for he had promised the Langfords that he would return.

Now everyone has gone, Aunt and Uncle are asleep and the house is quiet. *Almost* quiet, for after all the shaking, I swear I hear the boards sighing with relief. As for me, I am filled to overflowing with the joy of these Daft Days and the promise of a splendid New Year.

Sally Cohen

Not a Nickel to Spare

The Great Depression Diary
of Sally Cohen
Toronto, Ontario
July 8, 1932 – August 20, 1933

By Perry Nodelman

Sally's streetwise cousin Benny has complicated her life before, nudging her out of the comfort of her close-knit Jewish neighbourhood. And he's about to complicate things again when he takes her younger sisters to the Santa Claus Parade and Hindl starts yearning for a Shirley Temple doll. How will a poor family, living through the Depression and struggling to make ends meet, ever afford that?

Shirley Goodness

November 10, 1934

Benny spent the whole afternoon being annoying. After he made a dumb joke about how skinny I am and I couldn't stop myself from blushing, he said my face looked like a beet. If he wasn't my cousin I'd never speak to him at all.

But he isn't all bad, I guess, because he offered to take Molly and Hindl to the Santa Claus Parade next week. Of course it's his fault they want to go. He's the one who turned on the radio even though it was Shabbes today. Pa would have yelled at Benny if he'd seen him do it. The radio was tuned to CFRB and that program about Santa Claus's adventures on his way to Toronto from the North Pole was on, and Molly and Hindl were sitting there at the kitchen table colouring in the advertisements in some old newspapers, and they got really excited about the Parade. So Benny said, let's take them, and I agreed.

Now I'm wondering if it's really a good idea. Sure,

Hindl and Molly know that Santa doesn't bring presents to little Jewish girls like them. But they're just six and eight, after all. Won't it make them feel bad if they see Santa and know he won't be coming down *our* chimney on Christmas Eve?

November 14

This morning Sophie sent me upstairs to get her purse before she left for work. Just because she's the oldest she thinks she can boss everybody. Molly and Hindl were on the stairs, pretending to be Jack Frost and Eaton Beauty feeding hurryberries to Santa's reindeer, like they heard on the radio on Shabbes. They knew all the reindeers' names, too. They are so, so excited about the Parade, they hardly talk about anything else. It can't be a good thing, but I guess we're going to have to take them like we promised.

November 17

I guess I'm glad we went to the Parade, because it really was so much fun! We left early enough to get a good spot on University near College, right by the curb. While we waited for the Parade to come by, the girls pretended to be Eaton Beauty and Jack Frost again, and Benny helped them out by pretending to be a reindeer. He made such a loud beepy kind of noise that everyone in the crowd stared at us and I started to blush again. But then we heard a band playing "Hark the Herald Angels Sing" and everyone started to sing along as the band marched by us — even me. Of course I shouldn't even know the words — it really isn't very Jewish of me. But I learned them from one of the ladies at St. Chris and I just couldn't stop myself.

Then the floats started to come by. My favourite was Father Neptune's Court, with dancing fish and lobsters and Popeye the Sailor Man from the funny papers on his own rocking ship. Molly laughed and laughed at the snails and the frog symphony in the Sunny Meadow Court, and Hindl was in heaven when she saw Cinderella and her coachmen. Hindl loves the story of Cinderella — she calls herself Cinderhindl when Ma makes her dust the parlour every week before Shabbes. Benny said the best thing was the drum majorettes showing off their legs, but I know he just said it to make me mad.

After Santa and his reindeer went by and the crowd cheered and the Parade was over, Benny said it wouldn't take us very long to walk over to the big Eaton's downtown and look at the toys in Toyland. Sometimes I think he has no brains at all. The last thing poor Jewish girls like Molly and Hindl need is to go look at a whole bunch of expensive Christmas toys they can't ever have.

But once Benny said it, there was no way to stop it. The girls begged and pleaded and finally I had to give in.

We stopped outside Eaton's to look at the Christmas windows with all the toys and lights in them, and then we went inside and headed up the escalator to Toyland on the fifth floor. The store was full of kids and parents, but we pushed through the crowd and made it to the doll section.

After listening to the girls pretending to be Jack Frost and Eaton Beauty all week, I thought they'd be most interested in the Eaton Beauty dolls. They are really, really adorable this year, with shoes and socks you put on and take off, and cute lacy slips, and eyes that really open and close. But when Hindl saw the Shirley Temple dolls, she just stood there and stared and stared at them. I don't know why. She's almost the same age as the real Shirley Temple, but I don't think she even knows who Shirley Temple *is*. Hindl sure hasn't ever seen her in one of her movies, what with Pa out of work again and money being so short.

Hindl wanted to pick up a Shirley Temple and hold it. I would have let her, but there was a snooty store lady staring at us the whole time.

When Molly asked Hindl if she wanted a Shirley Temple, Hindl stared at the dolls a bit more and then said, "No, of course not, don't be silly, Molly. I already have a doll." She means my old doll. I'm glad I decided to give Matilda to Hindl last year so at least she *has* a doll, even if Matilda has a hole in one cheek and little cracks all over. And of course she never was anywhere near as cute as Shirley Temple. I knew we should never have gone to Toyland.

November 20

On my way to the toilet room I passed Molly and Hindl's room and Hindl was there by herself on the bed, making Matilda dance on the bedspread while she sang her a song I'd never heard before. It was something like this:

I like what you like, beans and oyster stew,
And I like what you like, on account'a I love you.

It was really cute. I asked Hindl what the song was, and she blushed and said it was a Shirley Temple song and Shirley sings it in a movie. She knows because her friend Ruthie at school told her all about it. Ruthie's parents took her to see that movie and Ruthie liked it so much that she made them stay and watch it *two* more times. She learned the words of the song and taught it to all the other Junior One girls and now they're all pretending to be Shirley Temple every day in the playground.

I guess that's why Hindl loved those Shirley Temple

dolls so much. I wish there was some way I could get her one.

November 22

While we were doing the supper dishes Hindl asked why Santa Claus never brought us any Christmas presents. Molly told her it's because Jews don't believe in Santa Claus. Hindl said she knows that, of course, but then she got quiet and frowny and I could tell she wasn't happy about it. I reminded her that we have Hanukkah instead and it's only a couple of weeks away and that if she was lucky she might get some Hanukkah *gelt*. Hindl said she knows that, too, but it isn't the same. Then she made me lean down and she whispered into my ear. She said she bet that if you were a Jewish girl and you wanted something really bad and you wished for it really hard, Santa might feel sorry for you and bring it to you anyway. She was thinking about those Shirley Temple dolls, I just know she was.

Double darn that Benny and his stupid Santa Claus Parade.

November 25

While Hindl was in the toilet room, Molly rushed down to my room and said she had to tell me something, but it had to be a secret. So I crossed my heart and hoped to die and promised I wouldn't tell anyone, and Molly said that she knows that Hindl really, really wants a Shirley Temple doll. I told her that wasn't a secret because I knew it already. But then Molly told me that *she* wants Hindl to have a Shirley Temple doll, too. Molly is a good sister, and she's right. Hindl is such a sweetheart. She deserves one of those dolls.

If I told Ma about it, and Ma told Pa, maybe they could find a way to buy it for her.

Oh, who am I kidding? Even doing odd jobs, Pa hardly makes enough to feed us, let alone buy an expensive doll. And anyway, if Pa knew Molly was expecting *Santa* to bring it, he'd have a conniption. There's no way I can tell them about it.

November 27

I talked to Sophie about Hindl and the doll. I know Sophie doesn't give Pa all the money she makes at Uncle Bertzik's factory because she has at least three different kinds of lipstick now. And she's the one who eats bacon, after all, so I thought she'd understand. Boy, was I wrong. She gave me a huge lecture about silly superstitions and how Christmas is so commercial nowadays and how she was glad we were Jewish so we wouldn't have to waste our hard-earned *gelt* on all that silly nonsense. What a killjoy.

But Sophie did have a suggestion. She said that if I

cared so much about it, why didn't I just earn some money and buy Shirley Temple for Hindl myself? Oh sure. All I have to do is figure out how to earn $5.50 — that's what the smallest Shirley Temple costs. $5.50! That's about four times more than an Eaton Beauty, and Eaton Beauties aren't cheap either. Sophie is *meshugge*.

November 29

Dora came home from work today carrying a big package, and she said it was for me because Sophie told her about Hindl and the doll. I got all excited and ripped it open, and what do you think it was? Not a Shirley Temple doll, that's for sure. It was just a big stack of men's overalls, the kind farmers wear, and the buckles to attach to them. Dora said she talked Mr. Tulchinsky into letting her bring them home to sew on the buckles as piecework, 5¢ a piece. She would take some and I could do the rest and we could earn the money for the doll. Dora is a sweetheart.

November 30

I wish I wasn't such a klutz at sewing. We got up early this morning and started on the overalls before Dora went to work and I went to school, but I only did two pairs while Dora did four, and then Dora said my stitches were too messy and we'd have to rip them out and do them over. I ripped the stitches out and tried again, and they were almost as bad as the first time, and Dora said never mind, she'd do them herself.

I feel rotten. Dora spends all day at work sewing. I can't let her fill up her spare time doing all those buckles. Ma would help her if I asked, but Ma is already run off her feet. Darn sewing anyway.

December 1

It was the first night of Hanukkah tonight. There wasn't any Hanukkah *gelt* again this year.

When Pa lit the first candle and said the prayer about how the Lord made miracles for our ancestors, I couldn't stop myself from thinking about the overalls and Shirley Temple. I need a miracle myself right now.

December 4

Gert and Chaim came over for dinner last night. Ma invited them because Auntie Rayzel gave her an extra chicken she had that needed to be cooked right away. Gert and Chaim are hardly ever here now that they have their own apartment, so I guess I was happy to see them. Gert hasn't pinched me even once since she married Chaim and moved out. After dinner Gert let us take the baby up to my room and Molly and Hindl and I took turns holding her. I love

Barbara even if her mother is as annoying as her father. Chaim is such a *schmendrick*.

When Gert came up to get Barbie, she saw the pile of overalls on the dresser and asked what they were, so I had to send Molly and Hindl away and then tell Gert about the Shirley Temple doll. When Gert heard about the sewing she said, "*You?* Sewing!" and she started laughing like crazy. What a way for a married woman with a baby to behave!

But after she finally stopped laughing, she said she thought she might have a deal for me. And she did, too! She said she'd do the buckles if I would babysit Barbie for her. Gert is even better at sewing than she is at pinching. I agreed right away!

December 13

Gert had to take Barbara to tea at Chaim's Auntie Becky's house this afternoon, so it's the first chance I've had to write anything all week. I've been at Gert's after school every day.

Looking after Barbie is fun most of the time, except when I have to change her diapers. When I brought Gert the overalls, she took them into her bedroom and I haven't seen them since. I hope she's working on them, but I don't know when — she spends all day looking after Barbie, and whenever I'm there she sits around looking at magazines or *kibitzing* with her friend Ida about movie stars. I guess I just have to trust her. I don't want to disappoint Hindl. Or Molly either.

December 15

Benny came over with a photograph of Shirley Temple for Hindl. He read in the *Star* that Eaton's was giving them away in Toyland, so he went after work and got one for her. Her eyes lit up when she saw it.

December 16

Boy, am I tired! I spent all day looking after Barbie. I must have changed her diaper about twenty times. After Chaim went over to Altman's with his loud-mouth friends, Gert said she was going to their room to work on the overalls, and she went in there and closed the door and I didn't see her or hear her for about two hours. I bet she was having a nap, not sewing at all.

December 19

I've asked and asked, but Gert won't let me see those overalls. I know she's been working on at least one pair, because when I went over there today she was sitting at the kitchen table with it and she made some comment about me not trusting her and I should be more grateful. But then Ida came over again, and by the time I left two hours later, Gert still hadn't finished sewing the first buckle on.

December 20

Still no sign of the overalls — I tried to sneak into Gert and Chaim's room while Gert was in the toilet room, just to get a look at them, but she came out too soon and nearly caught me.

When I got back home, Molly and Hindl were already ready for bed. When I went up to say good night to them, Hindl was holding Benny's Shirley Temple photograph like it was a baby she was cuddling, and singing to it about oysters and bean stew. And while Hindl was singing, Molly gave me such a look!

I'm getting that doll for Hindl even if I have to change two million diapers.

December 22

It's a disaster, a complete disaster! I *knew* I never should have trusted Gert. I went to pick up the overalls today so Dora could take them back to the factory and get the money, and Gert only had five pairs done! *Five!* She didn't even apologize, just complained about all the work she had to do with a young baby and all and what did I think she was, my slave? I could tell she felt bad about it though — Gert always yells at people when she's sorry about something.

Anyway, now Dora has to listen to Mr. Tulchinsky get mad at her because the overalls aren't done, and there's nowhere near enough money for Hindl's Shirley Temple, and Molly is going to be so upset, too. Even if she *is* sorry and even if she is my sister, Gert is a lazy @#$%#.

December 23

I spent all day moping around the house. Benny came over but all I could do was *kvetch* to him about the doll and Gert and the overalls and he said, "Enough complaining, already," and he left. So I went up to my room and closed the door and lay on my bed and felt sorry for myself.

But then Hindl came in and said I shouldn't be so unhappy and I could have Matilda to hold if I wanted, because Matilda always makes her feel better. She was right, too. Holding Matilda did make me feel better, even if I am fourteen and I would die if anyone found out. Especially Benny. Or Gert.

But then Hindl lay beside me and Matilda and cuddled her Shirley Temple photograph and talked about how Christmas was just two days away now and Santa must be packing up his sleigh. That made me feel even mopier than before.

What a day!

Before she left this morning, Dora told me I had to come and meet her at the factory after work. I was too mopey to go anywhere, but she begged and begged until I finally said I would. When I got there, she told me Mr. Tulchinsky was mad about the overalls, but she's used to that because he's always mad about everything. He gave her 40¢ for the finished ones, and she wanted to take me over to College Street and see what we could get for it. She said 40¢ is better than nothing, isn't it? And Hindl was expecting a present, so finally I said I'd go.

After looking in five different stores, we found a book of Shirley Temple paper dolls with four Shirley Temples in different kinds of undies and a whole bunch of outfits to cut out. It wasn't a real doll, but Dora said at least it was Shirley Temple, so I let her buy it even though it just made me mopier. Then Dora said we had just enough left over to buy some Christmas candy for Molly, so she wouldn't feel left out. It was nice of Dora, of course, but I thought it would just make the girls sad.

Boy, was I wrong! When we got home, Molly and Hindl were in the kitchen. Hindl squealed when she saw the paper dolls and hugged us and said they were lovely and they were just what she wanted. And

Molly gave me a big hug, too, and whispered thank you. Hindl didn't seem to care that it wasn't a real doll, but I think maybe it's because she's still counting on Santa.

Anyway, then Molly ran out of the kitchen and up to their room and came back with another paper doll for Hindl. She made it herself from a picture of Shirley Temple she cut out of an old newspaper and pasted on cardboard, and she drew the clothes for it all by herself!

When she gave it to Hindl she said "Merry Christmas," and Hindl said "Merry Christmas" right back. It's a good thing that Pa and Ma were over to Tanta Lena's and couldn't hear them.

Then Benny strolled in with a big box and gave it to Hindl and said "Merry Christmas" too. It was a *real* doll this time! Not a Shirley Temple doll, but a nice little doll anyway, even if its dress was a little stained. And Benny had made it a sash like beauty queens wear that said *Shirley Temple* on it in crayon. Afterwards, Benny told me his Ma found the doll in a second-hand store on Lippincott, and he got her to give it to him for Hindl and made the sash himself so that maybe I wouldn't *kvetch* so much.

And as if that wasn't enough, Sophie came home from work with a package for Hindl too! It was a book called *The Story of Shirley Temple* — imagine a little girl like that having a whole book about her! It wasn't a doll, and Hindl can hardly read yet, but Molly said she would help her. Hindl thanked Sophie, but she didn't say Merry Christmas. I guess Sophie is okay after all.

Hindl was telling Molly she could have one of the Shirley Temple paper dolls from her new book and Molly was sharing her candy with everybody when who should show up but Gert and Chaim — and they had something for Hindl too! I *knew* Gert felt bad about the overalls. They actually brought Hindl a *real* Eaton Beauty doll — except it didn't actually come from Eaton's. Chaim said he knows someone who knows someone who works in the warehouse and the doll just sort of fell off a truck. Trust Chaim.

For a poor little Jewish girl, Hindl sure did get a lot of Christmas presents. I hope Ma and Pa won't be upset when they see them. They're all from Jewish people, after all, so they're really not Christmas presents.

December 25

It's Christmas today. I was worried that Hindl would be upset this morning when she woke and found out that Santa didn't bring her the doll she wanted. Sure, she got all those presents — but not a single one of them was a real Shirley Temple doll. But when I went to look in their room, she and Molly were so busy playing with the presents they didn't even notice that Santa hadn't come.

When I went in, Hindl gave me a big hug and said she was full of Shirley Temple goodness, and when I asked her what she meant, she said it was like in the prayer they say at St. Chris sometimes.

I told her I didn't know what she meant, and she said, "You know, Sally. It goes 'Shirley Goodness and mercy will follow me all the days of my life.'"

Well, they sure were following her yesterday, even if Santa didn't come. I guess you don't have to have Christmas for people to show they care about you.

Josephine Bouvier

Blood Upon Our Land

The North West Resistance Diary
of Josephine Bouvier
Batoche, District of Saskatchewan

Le 31 décembre 1884 – le 20 novembre 1885

BY MAXINE TROTTIER

When the North West Resistance broke out, Josephine's family sided with Louis Riel. But the Métis forces that fought at Batoche faced yet more challenges after the battle itself. The Bouviers and others who decided to stay have been struggling to survive, and still they do not hold title to their land.

A Time to Rebuild

Le 10 décembre 1885

How our little Alexandre's illness worries us all.

So very weary after this long cold day of travel, but still I cannot sleep. I am certain it is because it is the first time I have stayed in another person's home. Madame and Monsieur Parenteau, Louise's cousins, are very kind to take us in, and generous, for they have little more than we do after the soldiers burned our homes last spring.

I should not dwell on the troubles. It is hard not to, though, especially since Monsieur Parenteau, who is nearly as old as Moushoom, insisted on asking a hundred questions after supper. He wanted every detail about the battle at Batoche, since he had been unable to fight himself. He has but one leg. Moushoom gave him those details, but I could tell how it bothered him.

No one said so, but I knew that we all would be thinking about home for a long while tonight, and if

Plus tard

Poor little Alexandre. I heard him coughing, and so went to Louise, who was in the kitchen with Madame Parenteau, making an onion poultice for his chest. Madame had nothing else at hand. Perhaps it is helping, since his coughing has lessened. I think the cold air did Alexandre no good today, even though Louise had him well bundled, and Papa drove the horses hard to get here quickly. Madame Montour's home in Prince Albert is still a good day's journey away. I am so worried about my tiny new brother.

Worrying about his cough does no good. I pray that journeying to Louise's sister at Prince Albert will.

Encore plus tard

No more coughing, and so it was not the coughing that has wakened me, but the snoring. Moushoom, Armand, Edmond, Papa, Monsieur Parenteau and, I suspect, Madame Parenteau, all snore horribly. In this small house you cannot escape the noise. If Adrian were here instead of back home in Moushoom's cabin at Batoche, it would be even worse. *Abain*, nothing to do but write.

Besides, I have got to thinking, which is not wise at this hour, but cannot be helped. It is something that Monsieur Parenteau talked about after Moushoom told the story of the battle. He said that we were not all that far from the place where Louis Riel and his companions had hidden for three days in a certain Madame Halcro's root cellar. Monsieur Parenteau explained how he himself had seen the sash that Monsieur Riel gave to Margaret Halcro in gratitude for her kindness. She would show it to us, if we wanted, and describe exactly what had happened when Monsieur Riel surrendered.

Papa said he would consider it, but I could tell from his face that we would not be stopping *chez* Halcro. None of us needs to be reminded of events that are still as raw as open wounds.

Le 11 décembre 1885

Prince Albert at last. I have not seen much of it yet, except for this house and what surrounds it, but still, even that much is amazing. There are so many people here, and so many wagons and sleighs. I can see the Saskatchewan River — the North Saskatchewan River — from this bedroom, since Monsieur and Madame Montour's house is not far from its bank. There are no buildings over on the north side, unlike here on the south bank where there are dozens of houses, stores and other places of business. Papa says we will see the town in time, but for now there are far more important matters. I agree. Nothing is more important than the health of little Alexandre. Papa and Monsieur Montour have already spoken to a doctor, who will be calling tomorrow.

Le soir

We said the rosary after supper with Madame Montour, her husband, their two young sons Jean Paul and Jean Claude, and their daughter Sophie. It is a good thing that Papa, Louise, Madame and Monsieur pray with their eyes closed, which spared them the sight of all the boys, including Armand, making faces at each other. Moushoom and Edmond were also spared, since they sat in the kitchen smoking their pipes, but I was not.

Sophie did not make faces — she is my age, and so knows better — but she did wink at me, as if to say how much older and wiser we were than our silly brothers. Perhaps Sophie and I will be friends, which would be a good thing, since we are to share her room while we visit here.

Très tard

Only a little coughing, but now there is wailing, as the Montours' newest child, Elizabeth, has colic, and so cries a great deal. And I will not even write about the snoring again, other than to say all these sounds woke both Sophie and me. What I will write about though, is a wonderful discovery. Sophie also keeps a diary! She has told me that she often writes in it late at night when she cannot sleep, and so here we both sit, pen in hand.

Now I am certain we will be friends.

Le 12 décembre 1885
Matin

The doctor has sent word that we are to expect him this afternoon. One of his patients has gone into a difficult labour, and he cannot leave her. I saw Louise fingering the medal that her sister Rose sent her so many months ago. She and Madame Montour both know about the dangers of childbirth, and so I knew it was the reason she did so. That and her worry for Alexandre.

I feel sorry for that woman who is in labour, and hope that she and her child survive. Still, my love for Alexandre is greater than any of that. I pray the doctor comes soon.

L'après midi

Madame Montour had visitors this afternoon, neighbouring women who not only came to see her, but to see us. One of them, a Madame Pascal, clucked her tongue over Elizabeth and Alexandre while shaking her head, which I did not much care for. She recommended a medicine called Mrs. Winslow's Soothing Syrup, which she had bought at a place called Clark's Drugstore, and she put a bottle of the stuff in Louise's hand. Madame Pascal swears by it, explaining that the medicine not only stops coughing and soothes colic, but it puts a little one right to sleep. Louise said she would consider it, and so did Madame Montour.

Later, after Madame Pascal and the other ladies were gone, Moushoom said that he did not like the smell of that Soothing Syrup. It smelled like laudanum, like the poppy drug, and nothing was worse than laudanum. He had known men who craved laudanum more than whisky, and so how could it be soothing for a baby? Alexandre should not take a drop of it.

I agree.

Le soir

Still no doctor, but he did send over a bottle of medicine by way of a man named Thomas Eastwood Jackson. Mr. Jackson — he is not Métis — also owns a drugstore. This bottle contained something called Dr. Fowler's Extract of Wild Strawberry. I could see that Louise was torn over which medicine to give

Alexandre. That was when Moushoom spoke up. My grandfather had been very quiet since we arrived yesterday, and so his outburst, and that he began to question Mister Jackson, surprised us all. *What was in this medicine? Anything bad?* The answer to that was no. The medicine contained exactly what its name said, and everyone knows that strawberries are good for you. This satisfied Papa, Louise and Moushoom, and so Alexandre was dosed. What faces he made! We all laughed.

Sometimes I think laughter heals more quickly than any medicine.

Plus tard

Sophie says that Mr. Jackson has a brother William who was at Batoche, the very man who was Louis Riel's secretary. Sophie had heard that William Jackson was sent to an insane asylum after his trial, but he escaped and fled to the United States.

Poor man. Perhaps he will find peace there.

Le 13 décembre 1885

Mass this morning was said by Père André at St. Anne's Church. The adults and the well-bundled babies rode over in the Montours' sleigh, but the rest of us walked. It was not a very peaceful walk, what with the boys pelting each other and us with snow.

It made me feel strange to see Père André after all this while. They say he was a great comfort to Louis Riel just before Monsieur Riel's death. I hope that is the truth.

Le 14 décembre 1885

Monsieur Montour goes to his general store every day after he takes Sophie to school. This morning, though, he left Sophie at home. He would explain to the nuns that there was sickness in the Montour house, and that his wife's sister and her family were visiting for Christmas. Sophie was needed at home. The good sisters would understand.

Last night I heard Madame Montour telling Louise about St. Anne's school and how expensive it is. She and her husband pay $15.00 a quarter, so that Sophie may attend. Then there are her clothes and such, which are specially made by a seamstress named Miss McGuire, for Sophie must look as stylish as the other girls. She is even learning Latin, and so Madame Montour thinks it is well worth the cost.

It is a little hard not to feel a bit of envy — I have only this one skirt and blouse and my good dress for Sundays — but Moushoom has always said that envy is like rust. It will eat you up if you let it, and as I have no wish to be eaten by anything, I will not give in to

Plus tard

The doctor has come at last! He is a small round man named Dr. Maxwell, who has an odd way of speaking French. Papa says it is because he is from Scotland, and that is the reason there seem to be so very many *rrr*s in his words.

Dr. Maxwell listened to Alexandre's chest. He prescribed a treatment of misting to ease Alexandre's breathing, but was certain that he did not suffer from croup. It was Louise and Rose, though, who needed to rest and strengthen themselves so that they could pass that strength on to their babies when they nursed them. I could see that this did not sit well with either woman. The doctor added that Louise and her sister should eat red meat and perhaps take a glass of port each evening. Both would enrich their blood. And quiet — they must have quiet, and a chance to visit.

Dr. Maxwell is not married, I was later told. I suppose that is why he thinks that quiet is easy to have in a house filled with two little ones, and with restless boys.

La nuit

Sophie dislikes Latin. She cannot see what possible use it will ever be to her. She has also said how lucky I am to have been educated at home. She envies me, and especially envies the fact that, unlike her, I do not have to be laced into a corset each day so that my school clothing will fit properly.

Papa, though. I could see that the doctor's words eased his mind, but I could also see that his pride was hurt. He says nothing, but not being able to provide for his family as he once could is hard to bear. It is why we are here, of course, as there is not ever enough food back at Batoche since the war. I pray that Adrian has enough to eat. My brother's Christmas will be a lonely one with only Moushoom's dog Moon for company. And I pray that in time we will get title to our land, the land for which we have suffered so very much.

Le 15 décembre 1885

Papa and Monsieur Montour have come to an arrangement. Papa told him that visiting was one thing, but that our family refuses to take advantage. The arrangement is that as long as we are here, Papa, Moushoom and Edmond will work at the Montours' store. Dear Papa. He is such a proud man.

It has been difficult for all of us to have lost almost everything we once had, and the loss made it even harder for Papa to overcome his pride and leave Batoche. The night before we left he said it was almost as though we were running away. Moushoom reminded us all that a wise person knows when it is a good time to run, but that we would not actually be running — our horses and wagon were too slow for that.

We all laughed. It felt so good.

Le 16 décembre 1885

Sophie and I have also come to an arrangement. We will help with as many of the household chores as possible, naturally. But we will also look after the boys, and take them on outings each day so that the house is quiet for at least a few hours.

Le 17 décembre 1885

Madame Montour does not bake. She buys her bread and cakes from the East End Bakery, and so this afternoon Sophie and I walked there with Armand, Jean Paul and Jean Claude. There was bribery involved, I fear, but promising each boy a penny for candy did keep them from throwing snow at us. On the way back, Armand showed the twins how clever he is by reading aloud the words on a poster in the window of a store. I wish he had not.

The poster advertised a dramatic entertainment that will be happening tomorrow evening. How the boys begged Papa and Monsieur Montour to be taken. None of us will be going though, because the entertainment is being put on by the police — those same North-West Mounted Police who fought our Métis soldiers at Duck Lake. Moushoom says bitterness solves nothing, but there is a limit. Besides, he doubts that the police could be very entertaining.

Plus tard

I am sure it is wrong of me to think this, and I would never say it aloud, but this household does not feel Métis the way ours does. Madame and Monsieur Montour are Métis, of course, but they rarely speak Michif at home, only French and English. Monsieur says that English is the language of business here at Prince Albert. Somehow that seems so sad.

Le 18 décembre 1885

Papa and the others brought something wonderful back to the house this evening, a large spruce tree. I have heard about Christmas trees, of course, but they are not the tradition in Batoche. Sophie and I were allowed to hang the glass ornaments, since we could be trusted not to break them. What fun the boys had stringing popcorn and cranberries. Papa and Monsieur Montour set candles on the ends of some of the branches, and carefully lit them so that we could all enjoy the sight for a few minutes. Even Moushoom enjoyed this, saying that it was much better than watching policemen leap around on a stage. That made all of us laugh.

Later Monsieur Montour showed us all something in today's newspaper. He had placed a new ad there, one that listed all the goods he sells in his store. He had bought two copies of the newspaper, so that Sophie and I could cut out the ads and paste them in our diaries.

MONTOUR BROS.,

TRADERS

GENERAL MERCHANTS
Have just received a large stock

DRY GOODS AND GENERAL GROCERIES

Teas,
Tobaccos,
Coffee,
Oatmeal
Sugars,
Canned Goods
Cal. Pears.

Clearing out the balance

Crockery

AND

Hardware,

AT COST

LAST NOTICE

After the 31st December all the old firm accounts will be handed over for collection.

Le 19 décembre 1885

I have now seen a Christmas card, as one arrived here today, sent from Monsieur Montour's cousin in Regina. On it was the picture of a large bearded man that Sophie says is Father Christmas. Jean Claude and Jean Paul explained everything to Armand about Father Christmas. Later Armand told me he did not believe a word of it. A monster like *googoosh* living under your bed is one thing, but a man coming down a chimney is just foolishness. I had to agree.

Le 20 décembre 1885

Mass at St. Anne's. Père André's sermon was one of goodwill and peace. Papa spoke with Père André afterward. It seems that the priest sends his prayers and good wishes with us to Batoche when we return. Sometimes I wonder about prayers. They are not always answered, and even when they are, the answer is not always the one you want. It makes me think about how Louis Riel and so many of the women of Batoche prayed for victory during the battle. So much is gone in spite of those prayers.

Le Boon Jeu has heard my prayers, though. Even after these few days here, Alexandre does seem a bit better. So does Louise. Maybe it is the medicine, and maybe it is the red meat and port, but I think there is more to it than that. Louise loves us, but I know she is happy to be with her sister again, if even for a short while. When she was alive, Mama always said that love can cure a great many things.

You were right, Mama, as always.

Le 21 décembre 1885

Sophie's brothers have each hung one of their stockings on the mantel above the fireplace in the sitting room. The twins said that we must do the same or we would miss out on the treats Father Christmas leaves.

Plus tard

I see that Armand has hung one of his stockings next to the boys'. Although he thinks that the business with Father Christmas and the chimney is foolishness, Armand does not believe in taking chances where treats are concerned.

Le 22 décembre 1885

Sophie and I have each hung one of our stockings next to those of the boys. She says it is only in fun, since it is her parents who place the treats there. I am not to say anything to the twins, however, since they truly believe in Father Christmas. *Abain.*

Le 23 décembre 1885

The weather is so mild, and Louise and her sister in such good spirits, they decided to dress the little ones warmly and accompany us on our walk this afternoon. Alexandre and Elizabeth seemed to enjoy being pulled along in the twins' sled, and for once all three boys were well behaved.

As we went along, Sophie pointed out the sites. Here was the Anglican cathedral, which oddly enough is built of logs, and here was the Hudson's Bay Company mill, and Mr. Jackson's drugstore.

Just then Jean Paul pointed out the police blockhouse. The day was suddenly ruined for me, as that was the building where Papa, Adrian and so many others were imprisoned after the battle of Batoche. When I told Moushoom about all this, saying that I believed the blockhouse should be torn down, he only laughed. That blockhouse still stands, he said, but then so do the Métis people.

Moushoom. How wise he is.

Later, though, he and Papa talked about our friend One Arrow, who is still in prison in Manitoba. It must be so hard for a man who has always lived in a teepee to be trapped in a stone building. I will pray tonight that One Arrow will soon be free.

Le 24 décembre 1885

There was no quiet in the house today, but no one seemed to mind. After all, Christmas is tomorrow!

Le décembre 25 1885
Christmas, weather mild

Christmas dinner was a fine one, with a goose that Sophie and I stuffed. Louise and Madame Montour prepared a Christmas pudding in the English style, which I must admit was delicious. And I have tasted an orange for the first time! How wonderful it was. As well as the oranges, there were hair ribbons in Sophie's and my stockings. Father Christmas somehow knew that my favourite colour is blue.

He left something very strange in the boys' stockings, a toy called a *bandelure*. When used correctly, the wooden *quiz* unwinds itself from a string that you place over your finger, and then pops up most amazingly. The boys have yet to master their toys, though. Louise says that the *bandelure* is also called a Prince of Wales toy, which made us all laugh. And when Armand said that if the prince has a *bandelure*, perhaps Queen Victoria also has one, we laughed harder than ever.

What a happy day this was!

Le 27 décembre 1885

Papa has decided that we will set out for home tomorrow after Mass. Although Adrian is capable of taking care of what remains of our property, his Christmas must have been a lonely one. What is more, Papa feeels the itch to begin rebuilding, and the only way that itch can be scratched will be with hard work.

I will miss Sophie and these kind people, but she has promised to write. Oranges taste wonderful, and Christmas trees are beautiful, but I do long for Batoche.

Le 31 décembre 1885, tard

We are home, and a complete family again. How good it was to see Adrian after so long. And Moon! He yelped and whined with joy to once more be with Moushoom. I knew that I had missed both the dog and my brother, but I had not realized how very much until I had to struggle to keep the tears from my eyes. The struggle was a short one, though, as contentment quickly took its place. And weariness, since we could not let this year end without a small celebration. To bed, Josephine.

Après minuit

It was the firing of Papa's rifle that woke me, one shot to the west to bid the old year farewell, and one to the east to welcome in the new year. What a sad and strange time it has been. So many changes. So much lost. I suppose the loss is why I had decided not to write about what happened yesterday, but then that would not be the right thing to do. A story needs its ending, even when the ending is not the sort you hoped for. And Moushoom did tell me to always write the truth.

So. We did stop at Madame Halcro's house, after all. It was another one of those moments where our family all seemed to be thinking the same thing, although none of us spoke it aloud. She was more than happy for a bit of company, and for word of the goings-on in Prince Albert. Then she offered to show us Monsieur Riel's sash, and even let each of us hold it.

When my turn came, I expected to feel simply wool. Instead — and I will only tell this here — I felt far more. It was as though something of Monsieur Riel had been left behind in that sash. I thought that I could almost feel his spirit, but now I wonder if I was feeling the spirit of the Métis people.

I suppose there is no answer to that, and perhaps none is needed. After all, who can say what will happen this new year of 1886. I can say that when Papa spoke of rebuilding a few days ago, it seemed to me that he was talking about more than a house and barn. Together once more in Moushoom's cabin, I feel that our family has already begun.

Eliza Bates

Brothers Far from Home
The World War I Diary of Eliza Bates
Uxbridge, Ontario
December 25, 1916 – December 25, 1918

BY JEAN LITTLE

*Eliza's brothers both enlisted to fight in World War I.
On the Home Front there were coal shortages, rationing,
heart-stopping news of soldiers missing or dead.
While praying for her brothers' safe return, and longing
for her very own friend, Eliza's greatest comfort was
the warmth of her exuberant and loving family.
But Christmas Day 1919 brings a new challenge.*

damaged. Mind you, nothing in the parlour was destroyed.

But I can't write the whole story down right now. Everything is too muddled and I can't sit still and write, especially when I am not at home. It should be fun staying here at Tamsyn's house, and it is now and then, but I am too upset, I guess. I keep wondering how the others are and wanting to be with them, and worrying whether some other disaster is happening to them and I am not there to know about it. We will be meeting for supper, but that seems years away. I miss Mother. I even miss Verity! I never dreamed I would miss her so much when she left home to nurse overseas, but today she seems farther away than before.

I think of Hugo too and want to tell him our dramatic story. Maybe he knows. People say those who have died watch over us. I wish I knew this for sure. I loved him so much that I can still barely think about him being killed at Vimy, Diary. But I can't write about that now when my mind is full of what happened just last night. Oh, Dear Diary, thank you again! I will treasure you all my life long.

Saturday, December 27, 1919
Tamsyn's house, bedtime

Mother says I am too melodramatic at times, but even she has to admit that this has been a dra-

explained. Otherwise I would go ahead and write the *whole* story down. But now Tamsyn is back, smelling sweet from powder and shampoo, and her mother says we must put out the light.

Tomorrow, Dear Diary, I will get back and not leave out a single exciting detail.

Sunday, December 28, 1919
After supper

The church was jam-packed with people this morning. Usually they come out in droves the Sunday *before* Christmas and then on Christmas Day, but the next Sunday lots of them stay home. Maybe they were so glad we were all alive. Maybe they wanted to hear Father preach. There is something in the Bible about a "brand snatched from the burning" and maybe that is how they see us. Even Tamsyn's family came, and they are Anglicans. She told me afterwards that it was the first time she had ever gone to a Presbyterian church.

I forgot to put in about Rosemary and Jack coming to get Roo. While Jack was hugging Roo so tightly that he yelped, Rosemary grabbed you, Dear Diary, and kissed you. That was after I told her how you had saved her precious child. She kissed me too, since I actually carried Roo out of the burning house. It *was* noble of me, as he was yelling and kicking the whole way. Maybe he was frightened. I was. But he just seemed mad as a wet kitten. They stuck around for a while, but then they took their blessed baby back to the farm. They offered to take me too, but I wanted to stay close to Mother and Father and our house. This is where I belong.

Father told us that the fireman said the fire started in the cellar, in one of the beams. The person who put electric wiring in was somebody in the congregation, and Father suspects he made a mistake. The fireman thinks the fire went up the wall into the chimney that led up into the old fireplace and then began licking its way along the wall. By the time I woke Father, there were flames and it had gone through to the kitchen. We are lucky the firemen came like a shot. There is smoke and water damage and a big hole in the one wall and everything stinks, but they say it can all be fixed.

Moppy was away visiting her sister over Christmas, but she came rushing back as soon as she heard the news. She wasn't happy to see how much would have to be cleaned up. It will make her usual job of keeping us tidy all the more difficult.

Belle was badly frightened by the whole thing and clings onto Mother's skirt all the time. Well, she *is* only seven. Charlie and Susannah strut about, bragging about their narrow escape, but now Charlie

Wednesday, December 31, 1919

Tonight is New Year's Eve. We should be celebrating but we are moving instead. I am going to be sharing a double bed with Belle. I do love my little sister dearly, but she is not a restful bedmate. Mother has promised that we will be going home in just two or three more days! I never realized how precious my own house is to me. My room seems like paradise. I don't mind a smell of smoke as long as I can be back where I belong.

I was just leaving Tamsyn's when Lavinia and her husband drove up in the station taxi. Her husband helped her out and she lifted the baby in her arms. I felt truly sorry for her. She is so pale she is almost grey and her eyes look sort of empty and blank, as though she has not laughed for weeks. She is also far too thin.

That baby really does scream. He made my ears ache. I darted forward before I had time to think, and held out my arms to take him. I felt sure Lavinia would never be able to make it to the house without dropping him. I found out later that Albert's father does not carry him because it seems to make him cry even more. Or that is what Lavinia thinks. She practically threw Albert at me and staggered off up the walk into her mother's waiting arms. David — Dr. Lewis —

followed with their baggage. He is tall and very straight and he did not smile or even look at me and the squalling baby.

I walked up and down with the baby while they all came and went with suitcases and things. Dear Diary, Albert is not a normal child. He is a noise machine with a knotted-up, purplish face, and fists like flying hammers. No matter how I wound the blanket around him, he got a hand loose and smacked me with it.

Then I remembered something I saw Mother and Moppy do when Belle was small and raising a rumpus. When nobody was watching, I took him and sneaked into our smoky kitchen and found the honey in the cupboard. It was not as easy to do as you might think with Albert clutched to my chest. I dipped my finger in and put a drop between his lips. It worked! For about ten seconds, he was busy sucking at the taste. My ears rejoiced in the small rest from the assault and battery of his crying. Before he got going again, I gave him another taste and, during the stillness, took the honey jar and put it into my coat pocket, making sure the lid was on tight.

When I came back out carrying Albert, who was making faces and getting ready to bawl again, Lavinia was standing in the snow looking frantic. You would have thought I was a kidnapper. "What did you do to him?" she shouted at me. But good old Albert let loose with his next bellow and drowned out any answer I might have made. I handed him over without having to mention why his lips were sticky. When I get a chance, I will tell Tamsyn the secret. It won't work a miracle, but it maybe will help for tiny bits of time. His cry is like a fire siren! Yet Lavinia hugged him to her as though she had snatched him from a lion's jaws.

I stood and watched her rush back inside with him and I admit I was pleased he was making an enormous rumpus. He wanted more honey.

After that, Tamsyn went over to Mrs. M's with me, glad to escape from the trouble at her own house. She told me more about Albert's father. He was going to start a general practice when he got home from the War, but Lavinia's getting Spanish Flu, and almost dying, changed him. Albert's birth might have helped set everything straight, but instead it made the whole thing worse.

Tamsyn says she is scared of David sometimes. When they have visited before, he has had bad dreams and talked in his sleep. When he wakes up, he is stiff and hard to talk to.

Nobody talks to Tam about what's wrong, but she has heard Lavinia pouring out her troubles behind closed doors. I told Tamsyn that David should talk to

Father. Everybody says he is wonderful with the men who come home from the War with troubles. So many are out of work because the jobs they had before they joined up are gone. Even the men who come back in good shape are having a hard time finding work, now that they're home.

Tamsyn said she did not think David would talk to a minister. He has told Lavinia he does not believe in God any longer. He is not the only one. I overheard Father tell one of the men that we all lose our faith in God once in a while, but it does not matter because God never loses His faith in us. Tamsyn looked shocked. "I never thought a minister would say such a thing," she said.

I said I needed fresh air and went outside. She did not follow me. I sat on the front steps and I thought about Hugo and wondered if he would have come home from Vimy like that, empty and cold inside. I miss him so and I would want him back home no matter how badly he was hurt. But how would he feel about life after what he had been through? He was always so strong and filled with laughter. Is it just another sort of war wound?

Jack's burns are so obvious, but does the hurt inside go deeper? I don't know. I need Hugo to explain it to me. And nobody talks about Hugo much these days because we are afraid of hurting Father. Jack and I do

Bertie smile, although nobody else seemed to notice. It was a real smile too, not just gas. But it didn't last. When he started yowling again, I headed back to Mother and Mrs. M and Belle who, when she cries, does it quietly.

I have written a lot because there is nothing else to do here. Mrs. M only reads religious magazines, too preachy for me. Belle and Mother finished the jigsaw puzzle and now I can hear Mother reading *The Five Little Peppers* out loud. Belle thinks Phronsie Pepper is just like her. I am glad that Mother and Father did not name *her* Sophronia. Sweet as Phronsie Pepper is, I much prefer the name Emily Belle.

Now Belle is coming to bed and I am tired too, so we will go to sleep early even if it is New Year's Day. I hope she doesn't kick tonight.

"Eliza, isn't it lovely to be together again?" she just said. Then she gave a gigantic yawn. She must feel safe with me, which is nice.

I have made a secret New Year's resolution. This year I will get my hair bobbed. I put it off because Hugo asked me to, but it is time I got on with grow- ing up, and short hair is the first step.

Friday, January 2, 1920

Father came over last night for dinner. We actually had goose. It was very greasy, but good. I told them all about Lavinia's troubles and Father took me apart to ask again about Dr. Lewis. Maybe he will drop in on Albert's father.

I told Mother I wanted to get my hair cut and she said she saw no reason why I shouldn't. The Bible calls long hair "a woman's crown of glory," but Mother says she thinks St. Paul would not have felt that way if *he* had had to look after such a crown. It is funny she says this, because her own hair is long, but I thought I wouldn't ask.

She actually made an appointment for me to get it done and suggested that I keep mum about it until the deed is done. That was what Verity did. Well do I remember! Sometimes it is handy to have an older sister to go ahead and blaze the trail.

So I will be going back to high school with short hair like everyone else my age.

Saturday, January 3, 1920
After supper

I did it. My hair is bobbed. My head feels pounds lighter and a bit strange, as though I lost part of my self with my hair. I wonder if anyone's head ever came loose and floated away. It feels as though it might. Tamsyn says I will get used to it in no time. I wish Mrs. M had a better mirror in the bedroom so I could gaze at myself without anyone watching me and making rude remarks. People can be so rude. Even Mrs. M has a certain way of smiling that makes me want to hit her. In books, they call that sort of smile "arch." I don't know why but I know I dislike it.

I personally think I look quite pretty, even with my one eye being slightly off.

No, I don't. I really think I look enchanting!

Bedtime

Finally, finally, finally! We are moving back into the Manse on Monday. We are pleased as punch. I went over today to get a book to read and found Dr. Lewis and Father dressed in old clothes, wallpapering the study. They were talking a mile a minute. I stood in the hall, as still as a shadow, and listened. Father was telling him that Uxbridge needed another doctor and this would be a good place to start a practice. David didn't answer, but he did not seem in a rage or anything. I crept away without saying a word. Father will help him if anyone can.

I could offer to lend a hand looking after dear little Bertie if the Lewises came here to Uxbridge to live. When they are not screeching, I do love babies. I love being left alone with them and smiling into their eyes. I pretend they are mine. I might even like twins — although perhaps I wouldn't. I don't remember much of ours when they were babies, except for Belle.

I might have known, Dear Diary, that the Preacher's Children would have to go back to school even on moving day. But Mother persuaded Father that we could come home at noon, and wrote us notes. That astonished us all.

The house smells so different, smoke and new wood and paint and plaster and soap and water. Also wallpaper paste maybe. It felt damp and cold too, until we got fires going in the fireplaces and Father started up the furnace. By the time we went to bed, Dear Diary, it was cosy. Don't you feel it?

Albert stopped crying today for three hours! He was awake and he actually gurgled. It must be the pram rides. Mother says it was bound to happen, but I still like taking some of the credit.

I went to Tamsyn's to return a cake plate her mother had sent over with a scrumptious roll jelly cake on it. And everyone seemed so peaceful. I took Bertie in my arms and walked up and down a bit and then I said I had to go and I walked over and held him out to his father.

Albert has more sense than they give him credit for. He put his arms out and went to his father and snuggled down. And Dr. Lewis smiled up at me and said, "Thank you, Eliza, for everything you have done to help us."

I was stunned, but I did not wait for more. I just ran for the door before the spell broke and dear Bertie remembered to yell. Yet my window is on their side of the house and I've not heard a peep out of him.

And at last, we are home again safe and sound. Even though we miss Hugo and Jack and Verity, it feels so good. We fit together like a stack of spoons. And again, thank you, Dear Diary, for saving us from the flames. We were always a loving family, but I think that on Christmas night we learned how much we really matter to one another.

Now to sleep in my very *own* bed by my very *own* self. What bliss! Rapture even!! At last, we are all together again, back where we belong.

Julia May Jackson

A Desperate Road to Freedom

The Underground Railroad Diary
of Julia May Jackson
Virginia to Canada West
January 3, 1863 – April 15, 1864

BY KARLEEN BRADFORD

Julia May and her family thought they had at last
found freedom when they made the final stage
of their dangerous trek north to Canada, but even here
old prejudices die hard, and the family has had
to search for a community that will truly welcome them.
As another Christmas in their chosen land approaches,
they still have no word of Julia May's brother Thomas,
who returned to the United States to fight
for the North in the Civil War.

Singing a Prayer

Friday, December 15th, 1865
Owen Sound, Ontario, Canada

We're in our own home! Papa and Mama finally saved up enough to buy a piece of land just under the cliffs on the east side of town, and Papa and Miles built us a little house. Lots of coloured folk live here on account of the shipyard being close by, and a lot of the men and boys work there. Papa's still at the stables though. He's so good with the horses, Mister Jones doesn't want him to leave.

It's a mite crowded with Sarah and Miles and baby Liza living with us, but we don't mind a bit, we are just so glad she found us and that we got some of our family together again. In any case, they're going to be renting a house right near us come spring, so Miles will be close to the harbour and his job on the steamers. For the first time in our lives we're in our own home! That's something for folks who used to be slaves down in Virginia only three years ago.

We worry about Thomas, though. Thought we'd hear from him soon after the war in the States finished in April, but we haven't heard from or seen him since he left to fight with President Lincoln's coloured troops. Good thing is, wherever Thomas is, he's not a slave anymore — not since President Lincoln set all the slaves free after the North won the war. He's a free man and can go where he pleases.

Folks say there's still a lot of confusion down there in the United States, both in the North and in the South, so we're praying and hanging onto the belief that that's what's keeping him away and he'll come back soon as he can. Then we can be a *real* family again. We won't even tolerate the thought that he's been killed.

Saturday, December 16ᵗʰ, 1865

My birthday! Mama made my favourite supper, chicken and dumplings, and Sarah made a cake with dried plums in it! I let little Aleisha help me blow out the candles on it. Fourteen of them. I'm surely getting grown up. Mama and Papa also gave me new mittens. My hands will be toasty warm now. Those old mittens were pretty ragged, especially since Boze chewed on one of them. He seemed to realize what he'd done and was real ashamed about it, and he's usually such a good dog that I didn't have the heart to scold him.

Monday, December 18ᵗʰ, 1865

This was quite the day. It started out just fine, but my goodness it didn't stay that way. Amelia came over this afternoon and brought me a bag of candies from Granny Taylor's as a present. That was good of her. Amelia is still my very best friend, even though I can't forgive her mother for what she said when I brought my mama to the white church. I don't want to go over to her house for milk and cookies anymore, and I used to *love* those molasses cookies her mother made. But now, if I tried to eat one of them, it would choke me. If they don't want my mama to be there, I don't want to be there either, no matter how much they like my singing. Anyway, I can sing all I want in our own church. Father Miller says I'm a "jewel in their crown."

But back to the candies. When we opened them, Joseph had his nose right in there and I had to share with him. Partly to get away from him, Amelia and I decided to go climbing on the rocks on the west hill. I haven't been up there very much since we moved over here to this side of the river. It was wet, but not snowy, so we figured it would be all right. We were wrong.

Boze came with us, as he usually does. When we got to the bottom of the cliff I told him to stay. He's always done just what I tell him to, but I don't know what possessed him today. I didn't realize it till too late, but he decided to climb up after us. Crazy dog. Those rocks are slippery and full of holes and cracks and no good place for a dog.

We'd just about got to the top when I heard yelping behind us. I knew right away it was Boze and, even though I couldn't see him, I could tell by the sounds he was making that he was in trouble. I had to get back to him fast. We climbed back down to him and, sure enough, he had slipped into a big gap between two rocks and he was stuck. I tried to reach him, but I couldn't. He was too far in and getting more and more frantic. I saw him pulling and pulling, but one of his back legs was caught. I was really afraid that he would break his leg, yanking on it like that, so I tried my best to calm him down, but nothing I said did any good. I was getting about as frantic as he was.

Finally I made a plan. I told Amelia I was going to lie down right at the edge and lean over into the hole. Told her to hang onto my feet so I didn't go in as well. At first she was too fussed to do it, but I didn't give her any choice. I was worried about Boze. I lay down, stuck my feet back and reached for him.

"If you don't hang onto me I'm going in!" I shouted at Amelia. I meant to scare her into grabbing my feet, but I suddenly realized it was the *truth*. Those rocks were so slippy and slimy with wet moss, I was sliding in and couldn't stop! Thank goodness she came to her senses in time and grabbed onto my ankles. Held on so tight I've got bruises all over them, but it did stop me from falling. I managed to reach Boze and work his leg out of the crack. Fool dog was so glad to see me he wouldn't stop licking my face.

Anyway, I finally got him loose and he clawed his way back up. Then I had another problem. How was I going to get back up?

"You've got to pull me up," I yelled to Amelia, but I was worried. She's not all that strong. But she did it. Got me far enough up that I could push against the sides with my hands and get myself the rest of the way out. I just sat there catching my breath for a minute. Boze was acting the idiot, jumping and leaping all around. I didn't know whether to be mad at him or glad he was all right. I guess I was both. Then, of course, we had to get back down. That was even harder than getting up!

Anyway, that ended our outing for today. I think maybe we'd better not be climbing around there again until next summer. And I'd better lock Boze up real good when we do go.

Friday, December 22nd, 1865

Christmas next week! I'm so excited. Christmas in Canada is wonderful! Mister and Missus Frost up at Sheldon Place bring a great big tree into their house and decorate it all up with fancy trinkets and candles. On Christmas Eve they light the candles on the tree and invite everybody, coloured and white, to come in and see it. Then folk come around singing carols and they give us all hot spiced cider to drink. It's usually snowing and it's really pretty. Last year Missus Frost sent us home with a fat chicken for our pot on Christmas Day, too. They are such good folks. But then, you'd expect that from people who built cabins on their own property for slaves who made it this far on the Underground Railroad, then let them live there until they can find a place of their own, like we did.

We won't have a tree in our little house, but we'll build the fire up extra good and Mama will fix us a fine supper. Afterwards, we'll go to our own church to hear Father Miller's Christmas sermon and sing carols. It will be especially nice this year because Christmas Eve is on Sunday and that means we'll have a Christmas service in the morning and another one again at night.

I love Christmas, but oh, how I wish Thomas was here — *when* are we going to get some word from him? This family has been torn apart for too long. Thank goodness we got Sarah and her family back, but Christmas always makes us think about Caleb and Daniel being sold off all those years ago. I don't think

Mama and Papa could bear it if we lost Thomas too. I know I surely couldn't.

And I miss Noah too, even though I'm glad there are two other coloured children in my class this year. I didn't like being the only one in our class after Noah left to work on his family's farm, but it's not just that. I truly do miss Noah.

Never thought I'd see the day when I said *that*, considering how he used to provoke me when I first met him. How things have changed! I'm still hoping he'll come back to school some day. For someone who's real smart and loves learning, it's a shame he left. I can't blame him, though. Those white boys made his life a misery. I don't know why people are so mean.

Saturday, December 23rd, 1865

Father Miller came round to our house. Sent Mama into a flurry, fixing tea and cakes for him, but he put her at ease. Complimented her on her cornbread. Said it was the best he had ever eaten. There's nothing like Virginia cornbread, Mama always says. Nobody up here in Canada makes it near so good.

Anyway, the reason he came round is because he wants me to sing a carol at the evening Christmas service. All by myself! At first I didn't know what to say, then I got real enthusiastic. We fell to deciding what I would sing. We finally settled on "Joy to the World." I love that carol. I just love singing it out as loud as I can.

Sunday, December 24th, 1865

Church this morning. I couldn't concentrate on Father Miller's sermon. Too busy thinking about singing tonight. Not really worried — everybody here is so nice. Mama's been working hard and she made me a brand new bright red dress. She braided my hair up around my head and Papa brought home a red ribbon for me for a Christmas present. I am going to look grand.

Later

How can I even begin to describe what happened at church tonight! I don't have near enough time, and I'm still too full to bursting with all the mixed feelings inside me. I think I'll just go to bed and hold it in my heart until I can find time to write about it properly.

Tuesday, December 26th, 1865

It's really late, everybody is asleep, and I can finally write what happened. I have a new candle beside me and I think I'll be using most of it up before I get everything written down.

Because it was Christmas Eve, we decorated up our house with evergreen boughs. I do love the smell of them in the house! Mama made us a good stew with lots of meat in it and Sarah baked up a storm while I minded the babies. Liza is walking all over the place now and I have to watch her real careful or she'll get into trouble. I never would have believed it, but Joseph is actually a help with her — she follows him around all the time and he doesn't mind a bit. Actually likes it. And our own little Aleisha is beginning to toddle around and she's determined to follow him too. Keeps him busy, especially when it's too cold to take them outside. It's right amusing to watch him with those babies.

Missus Frost sent over a roasting chicken for us to have on Christmas Day, even though we don't live on their property anymore. That was generous of her, and it certainly was welcome, especially for the reason I'm going to write about.

After our supper we went back to the church. It looked so beautiful from the outside, with candles glowing in the windows and frost making pictures that looked just like fine lace all around them. Father Miller didn't give a regular sermon, just recited the Christmas story. We all sat so quiet. Sarah held Liza with Miles beside her, and I could see tears in her eyes when Father Miller came to the part about the Wise Men bringing gifts to the baby. I was almost crying too, but my stomach was telling me to get nervous about singing all by myself, so I didn't.

We sang hymns and carols, and everyone was in the spirit and clapping and having a wonderful time. Then Father Miller came over to where we were sitting and led me up to the front by the hand to sing *my* carol. I stood there, took a deep breath, and just let that song roll out, loud as I could. All my nervousness melted away. I could feel myself filled with the joy of it.

Then suddenly the door opened and somebody walked in. Everybody turned to see who had come so late. It was a boy in a dirty, tattered blue soldier's uniform.

At first I thought it was Thomas and my heart gave a lurch. I stopped singing right in the middle of the last verse. Then I realized it wasn't him and I near burst into tears, but the next minute I saw it was Jeremiah, that boy who persuaded Thomas to go down South with him to fight with the Union Army. If he was there, I thought, he must know *something* about Thomas! I couldn't help myself, I just raced down the aisle toward him. I saw Mama and Papa give me a horrified look, then they saw who it was and they ran at him too. What a commotion! Everybody in the church got up from their seats and poured around us.

"Jeremiah!" Papa shouted. "Is Thomas with you?"

Jeremiah just shook his head. At the look on his face, everything went real quiet.

"He's not dead," Mama cried. "Oh, Jeremiah, tell me he's not dead!"

Jeremiah just shook his head and for a moment he couldn't seem to speak. Mama's knees suddenly gave way, and Papa grabbed onto her to hold her up, but he was shaking bad as she was.

Finally Jeremiah spoke. "No, ma'am," he said. "He's not dead, but he is wounded. Wounded bad, I think. Last I saw, they were carrying him off the battlefield to a hospital tent somewhere. When the fighting was all over, I tried to find him, ma'am. I tried the best I could, since I'm the one got him to go back there with me in the first place. But I couldn't. Figured the best thing I could do then was find you folks and tell you."

Father Miller came down the aisle and held out his hand. "Welcome, son," he said. "Welcome back from the war. We're mighty glad to see you." Then he turned to me. "Come on, girl," he said. "You've got a song to finish."

Well, I did not think I could sing another note. My mind was just all jumbled up and I didn't know whether I was happy or not. All I could think was, Is Thomas still alive? And if so, where is he? Why hadn't he come back, too? What if he died from his wounds?

But Father Miller put his arm around my shoulder

and led me back up to the front. He started in to singing where I had left off and I couldn't do anything else but join him. My voice shook and I had to hold myself tight to keep the tears back, but with Father Miller's arm around me I got myself together. I wasn't singing with the joy I had been feeling before though. I was singing a prayer.

I'm just too plain worn out to finish this now. I'll save the rest of the candle after all and finish this up tomorrow.

Wednesday, December 27th, 1865

Jeremiah came home with us for Christmas dinner, but he's going back to Toronto. Says he has a better chance of getting a job there, and he wants to be there when Thomas comes back, to tell him where we are. He's sure when Thomas finds out we're not in Toronto anymore, he'll go to Reverend Brown, at the church where we used to go, and Jeremiah will find him there.

Mama doesn't want him to leave. He's so tired and worn, she can't bear the thought of him making that trip back through the cold and the snow, but he's determined. I think Mama feels closer to Thomas while Jeremiah's here, but Papa agrees he should be in Toronto when Thomas gets there.

If he gets there. Nobody is saying it, but we're all

thinking the same thing. What if he didn't get better from his wounds? What if ...?

But I won't believe that. I refuse to believe that.

Thomas *is* alive and he *will* come back to us.

That will be our very own miracle. I know it.

This family has been through a powerful lot, but tonight we all sat around the table and linked hands, and thanked the good Lord for His blessing. Papa added a prayer for Thomas and for Daniel and Caleb. We've never heard anything more about them since they were sold off, and maybe we never will, but wherever they are, if they are still alive, they are free men. There's no more slavery in the United States of America, and there never will be again.

Even so, we won't be going back. Canada is our home now, and it's a good one.

Go to www.scholastic.ca/dearcanada for information on the Dear Canada Series — see inside the books, read an excerpt or a review, post a review, and more.